T0163444

THE BAILEYS HARBOR
BIRD AND BOOYAH CLUB

Terrace Books, a trade imprint of the University of Wisconsin Press, takes its name from the Memorial Union Terrace, located at the University of Wisconsin–Madison. Since its inception in 1907, the Wisconsin Union has provided a venue for students, faculty, staff, and alumni to debate art, music, politics, and the issues of the day. It is a place where theater, music, drama, literature, dance, outdoor activities, and major speakers are made available to the campus and the community. To learn more about the Union, visit www.union.wisc.edu.

THE BAILEYS HARBOR
BIRD AND BOOYAH CLUB

Dave Crehore

TERRACE BOOKS

A TRADE IMPRINT OF THE UNIVERSITY OF WISCONSIN PRESS

Terrace Books
A trade imprint of the University of Wisconsin Press
1930 Monroe Street, 3rd Floor
Madison, Wisconsin 53711-2059
uwpress.wisc.edu

3 Henrietta Street
London WC2E 8LU, England
eurospanbookstore.com

Printed in the United States of America

Library of Congress Cataloging-in-Publication Data
Crehore, Dave.
The Baileys Harbor bird and booyah club / Dave Crehore.
    p.   cm.
ISBN 978-0-299-28670-5 (cloth : alk. paper)
ISBN 978-0-299-28673-6 (e-book)
1. Door County (Wis.)—Fiction.   I. Title.
PS3603.R456B35   2012
813'.6—dc23
2011043964

This is a work of fiction. All names, characters, places, and incidents are either products of
the author's imagination or are used fictitiously. No reference to any real person is intended
or should be inferred.

Here's to the past, and the years that have fled,
Here's to the years that are lying ahead.
But better by far, if the truth we confess,
Here's to today, which is all we possess.

Thornton W. Burgess

Contents

The Baileys Harbor
Bird and Booyah Club

Back Home Again in Baileys Harbor

As anyone over sixty will tell you, growing old isn't for the faint of heart. But it beats the alternative, and so we submit to the passing years with all the grace we can muster.

This is a book about George and Helen O'Malley, who are growing old as gracefully as possible in Door County, Wisconsin. They're people you'd like to know and would be happy to have as neighbors. Retirement hasn't slowed them down very much, and things still happen to them—good things, mostly—although there are thorns in the roses sometimes.

Opposites attract, and George and Helen are a volatile and potentially explosive mixture of Irish and Norwegian. But they're still happy with each other, and glad to be jogging along side by side. Their fortieth anniversary is behind them now, and they wouldn't mind hanging around for another forty.

In case you're wondering, Door County is the stony, peninsular thumb of Wisconsin that sticks out into Lake Michigan, about sixty miles from Forestville to Rock Island as the herring gull flies. George and Helen were born there, and now they are back after thirty years of making a living in Chicago.

They grew up in the fifties, when the tourist invasion of the county was just beginning. George's family lived in the town of Baileys Harbor, on the east shore. His father ran a gas station, and was at one time the only man in Door County who could rebuild a

Ford V-8 in one long Saturday, with George standing by to hand him wrenches.

Helen, née Sorenson, lived on the family farm and cherry orchard near Peninsula Center, a couple of miles to the west. She was an only child, and her mother died young, so Helen had to cook and bake and keep house for her father when she was only a girl, and did a man's work in the fields as soon as she was able to reach the foot pedals of the old Case tractor. When she had a minute to spare she learned the names of the birds that nested on the little farm, consulting a copy of A Field Guide to the Birds that she bought with her egg money.

Helen was—and still is—slender and Scandinavian and easy on the eyes. The years have been kind to her, and she would be called elegant if she were a little taller. Her hair was—and still is—a corn-silk blonde, although she allows some gray to lighten it, now that she is in her sixties.

George is dark and Celtic. He stands an inch taller than Helen, and his curly salt-and-pepper hair is thinning a little. He has a cynical Irish sense of humor that makes him easy to live with, and a healthy skepticism that makes him reasonable. His talents are various: literary, musical, and practical. His writing has a certain simplicity and directness that editors like, he plays a mean viola, and if you need help fixing anything from a split infinitive to a fuel pump, George is the man to see. If you need sympathy, talk to Helen. She'll listen, and understand, and give you a little plate of something just out of the oven.

George and Helen went to high school together but paid no particular attention to each other until September 1961, when they were sophomores at the University of Wisconsin in Madison. A raft of ducks and a bag of sticky buns and a sparrow brought them together.

George was bird-watching at Picnic Point when he saw a girl in faded jeans and a red and black Buffalo plaid shirt on the path ahead of him. She was looking through binoculars at a flock of ducks on Lake Mendota. George raised his binoculars, took a quick look at the ducks, focused on the girl, and was surprised to find she was someone he knew.

"It's Helen Sorenson," he thought, and walked toward her, trying to come up with something brilliant to say. He stopped ten feet from her and opened his mouth, but nothing happened. So he turned and silently studied the ducks, hoping desperately that Helen would break the ice.

Eventually she did. "They're scaup," she said, "but are they the greater or the lesser ones?"

After a year of college and a five-credit field ornithology course, George knew a little of this and a little of that, but quite a bit about birds. It didn't occur to him that he was being tested.

"Lesser," he replied. "See the one that's stretching its wing? The white stripe on the trailing edge is only a couple of inches long. The greater scaup has a stripe like that, too, but it's almost the whole length of the wing. The shape of the head is a giveaway, too—the lesser's head is higher at the back . . ."

George realized he was babbling. He lowered his binoculars and turned toward Helen. Their eyes met.

"George?" she asked.

"Helen?"

"Fancy meeting you here," Helen said, and smiled. "I must say, for a kid from Baileys Harbor, you certainly are a font of information about scaup."

"Sorry about that," said George, "but I always get rattled in the presence of a beautiful woman."

Helen looked back at the ducks. "I'll keep that in mind if one comes along," she said.

When they got to the end of the point they sat on a fallen log and talked about their classes and watched the lights come on in the campus buildings across the bay. George regained his courage.

"Would you like to go birding in the morning?" he asked. "It's Saturday."

"Sorry," Helen replied. "I've got a paper due and it will take all weekend to finish it. But we could have breakfast on the Union terrace, and watch the sparrows. Say about seven?"

George was there early. When Helen arrived she was carrying a thermos and a grocery bag. "I've got eggshell coffee the way my dad likes it, and sticky buns. Hope you're hungry because there's a dozen."

The buns were still warm, fragrant with cinnamon, dripping with melted brown sugar, and covered with pecans. George ate two of them while he was waiting for his coffee to cool.

"These buns are poetry," he said. "Where did you buy them?"

Helen laughed. "Buy them? I couldn't afford to buy them. I made them. There are three of us girls in an apartment and I have access to an oven. They're still warm because I was able to find a parking place on State Street and I didn't have to walk very far."

"You have a car? My God, Helen, any woman who can make buns like these and has a car to boot needs a bodyguard. I volunteer."

Helen smiled, rolled up the bag, and handed it to George. "There are seven left," she said. "That should last you to lunchtime. Say, do you know how to change the oil in a '57 Ford Fairlane with a six?"

"Sure," said George. "I'll swap you an oil change for the buns."

Helen tore a page out of one of her notebooks and wrote a phone number on it. "Give me a call and we'll figure out a time to do it," she said. "Gotta go!"

George watched Helen until she disappeared into the Union. He noticed that all the other men on the terrace were watching her too. He opened the bag and took out another sticky bun. A light morning breeze arrived and rocked the sailboats at their moorings. A house sparrow landed on the table and began picking up crumbs; George tore a piece off the bun he was eating and held it out to the sparrow. The bird cocked its head, grasped the morsel, and began to peck at it.

"Good, isn't it?" George said to the sparrow. And he thought: "O'Malley, you're on to something here. She can bake, she likes birds, she looks like a blonde Ingrid Bergman, and she knows how many cylinders she's got. Don't screw it up."

From inside the Union, Helen watched George feed the sparrow. "It eats right out of his hand," she thought. "He's the one for me."

Helen's father had helped her buy the Fairlane so that she could come home more often, and George started riding back and forth with her, chipping in a couple of bucks for gas and sharing the driving.

George enjoyed Helen's company and the long talks they had as they drove. He had never been truly "serious" about a girl, but as the months went by he began to feel lonely and at loose ends when Helen wasn't around, and he wondered what that meant. Then, in February of '62, a blizzard changed their lives.

They were driving back to Madison on a Sunday night, and the farther south they went, the harder it snowed. Near Fond du Lac, they started slamming into drifts. The Fairlane slewed wildly in the wind, its rear tires whining. George spotted the neon sign of a roadside motel and pulled into the parking lot.

Rooms $12, the sign said. They had about fourteen dollars in cash between them. The thought of sharing a room occurred to them, but they stared straight ahead and didn't talk about it.

"I've got my checkbook," Helen said. "You could pay cash for a room and I could write a check for mine, but I don't dare. If I write a check to a motel, the people at the bank in Sturgeon Bay will see it. I know those people, and my dad does too. The gossip would be awful. Do you think we could just keep on driving?"

"We'd better not," George said. "We might get stuck and spend the night in a snowbank. It'll be safer to sit here and wait for the plows to come through."

The manager of the motel hadn't noticed them. The neon sign winked out, and Helen reached into the backseat for an old goose down comforter she kept there in the winter. It was a small comforter and they had to sit close together. Luckily, the Fairlane had a bench seat, and the gearshift was on the steering column.

George put his arm around Helen, and she rested her head on his shoulder. For a full quarter of an hour they watched the snow swirling down. Then George kissed her, and she kissed him back with surprising ardor. There was more snow and more silence.

"Penny for your thoughts," said Helen.

George knew what he wanted to say, but not how to say it. He opened his mouth and words came tumbling out. "I would like to keep on kissing you for the rest of my life."

"OK," Helen whispered.

There were a few more minutes of silence. Then he kissed her again, and they both laughed in sheer relief. By the time the first southbound snowplow went by about five in the morning, the windows of the Fairlane were iced up on the inside and George and Helen had reached an understanding.

George majored in journalism and Helen in elementary education. They graduated in June of '64, and two weeks later a judge in Sturgeon Bay married them. George landed a reporting job on a half-pint daily newspaper in southern Wisconsin, and Helen taught second grade. Pickings were slim at first; between the two of them they made just enough to eat and pay the rent and put gas in the Fairlane. But George was a good and entertaining writer, and stories with his byline began to show up in slick-paper magazines. Some months the magazines paid more than the newspaper.

One day in 1968, he heard through the grapevine that a copy-desk job was open on the *Chicago Sun-Times*. He didn't like big cities and preferred writing to editing, but the Fairlane needed a valve job and he was about to become a father. So he filled out an application, pulled together copies of his best work, and sent them off. A month later he had the job, and he and Helen moved into an apartment in Evanston just in time for the birth of their son, Bill. In 1997, Bill became William O'Malley, PhD, assistant professor of English at Northwestern University, and married Josie McConnell, RN, the red-headed colleen next door.

Helen inherited the Sorenson farm when her father died, but she couldn't bear to sell it. She kept up with the taxes by renting the plow land to neighboring farmers. When she looked at the 2000 tax bill, she was astounded to find that the land had grown a hundredfold in price since the 1940s.

"The fair market value is four thousand an acre, George," Helen said. "We're rich!" And on the strength of that, George retired from the copydesk and Helen decided that thirty-six years of second grade were enough for her.

For a long time the two of them had hoped to return to Door County, and they began to look for a place to live. It wasn't easy; while they had been working for newspaper and schoolteacher wages, people with serious money had been buying real estate. By the time George and Helen began shopping around, much of the best land had long since been sold off to developers. Prices were high on what was left, so high that a comfortable new house with a view would cost twice their net worth, including the Sorenson farm. They weren't as rich as they had thought.

"The last thing we need at our age is a six-figure mortgage," said George, "assuming we could get one in the first place. Hell, we can't even afford to build on your dad's land. It looks like we'll have to stay in Evanston and pay rent."

But they were entitled to a little good luck, and when they had almost given up the search, they found a property that no one else wanted at the end of a dead-end road. Coot Lake Lodge, it was called, a big log cabin that had been a country tavern, on the shore of an obscure and weedy ten-acre pond just north of Baileys Harbor. Another ten acres of swamp, bogs, and wooded glacial hills came with it, and they signed the papers and paid spot cash without a moment's hesitation. To buy in haste is to repent at leisure, but the O'Malleys have no regrets. The lodge is their home, and it's where we find them as their adventures begin.

Don't Get Old before I Do

///

*T*he sweet scent of burning popple filled the living room of Coot Lake Lodge. George knelt in front of the cavernous fieldstone fireplace, poking at some freshly cut logs that were grudgingly beginning to burn. It was the first Friday of July, but the week had been cold and rainy, and Helen had suggested a fire to drive out the damp.

She was busy in the kitchen. "The damn flue isn't drawing again!" George shouted to her. He crossed the room and went out the front door. From the rocky quarter acre that served as the lodge's front yard, he could see that no smoke was rising from the chimney. He shook his head in irritation, but then stepped back a few feet and gazed affectionately at the lodge.

"Oh, you've got your faults, but you're all mine, you big beauty," he said. And with some allowances for a century of wear and tear, the old tavern was beautiful in its way: two stories of native white cedar logs, fitted so precisely that only a little chinking was needed. On warm days it smelled faintly of spilled beer, and a neon Old Style sign still hung over the door. The day they moved in, George flipped the switch to turn on the sign and discovered that "Old" would light up but "Style" was burned out. They thought about taking the sign down, but in the end they kept it.

"Suits us to a T," Helen said. "Lots of age, not much style."

Coot Lake itself remained wild and unspoiled, largely because the wetlands that surrounded it had stymied the real estate speculators. Choked with lily pads, stunted bluegills, and nondescript waterfowl, it was named in the 1850s by a surveyor who stumbled out of the woods and said, "I came across a little puddle back in there somewhere, but I don't know if I could find it again. It's full of coots, shitepokes, and mud hens."

Back in front of the fireplace, George took off his ball cap and began to wave it at the smoke. Helen came out of the kitchen and joined George at the hearth.

"Well, it smells better than your pipe, but not that much better, George," she said, and twisted the cast-iron knob that opened the damper in the flue. Helen always closed the damper to keep out the bats that lurked in the chimney, and George always forgot to open it until smoke from the fireplace stacked up like storm clouds near the high-beamed ceiling.

Helen held her palms toward the fire. Now that the damper was open, flames began to lick around the logs, and the crackle of burning bark accompanied the steady hiss of sap boiling out of the wood. Their golden retriever, Russell, who had been lying in front of the fire, moved a few inches to avoid the sparks.

"You know why I always burn green popple, Helen?" George asked. "It's because . . ."

"It's because that way you don't have to carry water."

George looked at her and smiled. "How'd you know that?"

"Because I've heard that old joke a hundred times," said Helen. "You tell it every time you light a fire in the fireplace. Every single time. But the truth is, you burn green popple because you're too cheap to buy oak."

She sat down on one of the faded sofas that surrounded the fireplace. "George, I've been meaning to talk to you, and this is as good a time as any. Sweetheart, you're beginning to act like an old man sometimes, and you're the same age as I am, and I'm not old."

She picked up a supermarket tabloid from the sofa and opened it to a middle page.

"There's an article in here called 'Seven Signs Your Husband Is Becoming an Old Fogy,' and it says the first sign is forgetting things—like opening the damper, for instance."

"Yes, but . . ."

"No buts," Helen said, and turned the page. "Sign number two is

11

telling the same old stories over and over. Now you can't deny you do that, George."

"I'm not telling them over and over, I'm perfecting them. You know, there's a kind of a rhythm to a good story, and . . ."

"I don't doubt it," said Helen, "but for heaven's sake, think up some new ones. Your old stories are as good as they're going to get.

"Anyway, the third sign is pinching pennies, and burning green popple is exhibit A of that. And the fourth sign is starting sentences with phrases like 'I remember,' or 'Years ago,' or the real clincher, 'In my day.' You're doing that more and more, George. You're living in the past."

Russell sensed trouble and looked mournfully at them. Feeling a need to comfort someone, he rose from his spot by the fire, jumped onto the sofa, and laid his head in Helen's lap. George knew there was no point in further argument when his own dog had deserted him, but the rules of good-natured marital bickering required a response of some kind.

"OK, maybe I repeat my stories and forget to open the damper, but so far I haven't turned into a potted plant. And anyway, you only mentioned four of the seven signs. How am I doing on the other three?"

"Never mind," Helen said, blushing slightly. "I'll let you know if they get to be a problem."

Knowing she had won, Helen offered an olive branch. "You're still my sweetheart and you're still the best-looking Irishman in Door County, but don't get old before I do, all right? And do me another favor—dust off that trophy of yours on the mantel. The cobwebs are about to tip it over."

She squeezed George's shoulder affectionately and returned to the kitchen to finish breading the bluegill fillets and slicing the potatoes she was making for supper. George picked up the trophy and gave it a wipe with his handkerchief. It was a two-inch square of black marble topped with a little golden man, an impossibly slim and handsome young man pointing a plastic shotgun. George had won it three years before at a small skeet tournament in Green Bay.

He gave the engraved brass nameplate an extra rub with the handkerchief. "George O'Malley, Sub-Senior 20-gauge Champion," it read. There had been only one 20-gauge shooter in the sub-senior age class that day—himself—but a trophy was a trophy.

George looked around for Helen's newspaper, but she had taken it with her. He sat down next to Russell and threw a companionable arm around him. "Ah, well, old puppy, it's a great life if you don't weaken," he said, and began to fill his pipe. Russell sighed. He had heard that one before.

While Helen finished frying the fish and potatoes, George set their places on the long mahogany bar by the west windows that overlooked the lake. Helen brought in two heaping platters, and they started eating the potatoes with their fingers and dipping the bluegills in tartar sauce and melted butter. Little was said until the last bit of fish was gone. George poured a cup of coffee.

"Any news from town?" he asked. "Town" was Baileys Harbor, where Helen did most of the shopping.

"Not much, but I ran into Bump and Emma at the store, and Bump said to remind you about the Sturgeon Bay Open next weekend." Bump Olson was the local septic tank pumper, and he and his wife, Emma, were George and Helen's nearest neighbors on Coot Lake Road.

"For God's sake, Bump knows I wouldn't be caught dead playing golf."

"It isn't a golf tournament, it's a bass tournament." Helen got her purse from one of the sofas and pulled out a brochure. "According to this, the Business Boosters are holding it in Sturgeon Bay, and it's going to be just like the professional tournaments—catch and release, and a digital weigh-in at sundown. Bump said you should enter and show some community spirit."

"Spirit I got, money I ain't. And I'm not sure I believe in competitive fishing. It's a whatchamacallit—an oxymoron."

"A what?"

"You know—a contradiction in terms, like military intelligence or jumbo shrimp. Anyway, what's it cost?"

"It's only ten dollars," Helen said, "and there are some special divisions—junior, senior, fly fishing—with trophies for first, second, and third."

Trophies? That got George's attention. He looked over at the little golden man with the shotgun. Was he lonely? Would he like a little golden pal with a fly rod?

Helen brought in two dishes of ice cream, and the conversation moved on. But George kept glancing across the room at the little golden man. "Old fogy, eh? We'll see about that," he thought.

Later that evening, when Helen had gone to bed and Russell lay snoring before the dying embers of the fire, George rummaged in the lodge's dimly lit basement. In a corner full of discarded canoe paddles and torn landing nets he found what he was looking for: a faded brown leather tube, a canvas bag, and a telescoping aluminum push pole. He tiptoed up the stairs and put the tube and the bag and the pole on the bar.

The tube held a heavyweight three-piece, nine-foot bamboo fly rod intended for big pike and muskies. His father had bought it for a Canadian fishing trip that had been canceled by World War II. In the bag were an old Pflueger fly reel and a tin box of brightly colored flies and streamers his father had tied sometime before Pearl Harbor.

Rubbing its metal joints on the side of his nose to oil them a bit, George put the big rod together. The tip section had a slight twist, but it was sound otherwise. He took the rod outside and executed some false casts. It had a ponderous, powerful feel and made satisfying hissing sounds as he whipped it back and forth.

The reel, too, was still in good shape and the moths had left the flies alone. All he needed was a floating fly line heavy enough for the big rod and the tournament's senior fly-fishing trophy would be his! He knew the waters of Sturgeon Bay like the back of his hand, especially the Sawyer Harbor shallows, which were so treacherous that big-time bass fishermen with their giant boats and motors rarely dared to enter them in low-water years.

But George's sixteen-foot johnboat, shoved along by the push pole, would negotiate the shallows with ease. And among the boulders and stumps prowled Marilyn, a huge smallmouth bass he had already hooked and lost twice on bait-casting tackle. He called her Marilyn because, as he had once told Bump, "She's built like a brick shithouse and she's got a lot of class."

George filled his pipe and looked out the window at the moonlight shining across Coot Lake. Life was sweet.

Life soured a bit the next morning in Green Bay, when George found that the fly line he needed cost more than fifty dollars. But he thought of Helen's warning sign number three and slapped down his credit card. "Penny-pincher, eh?" he muttered. Deep in the belly of George O'Malley, competitive fires that had smoldered for years were flaring up.

George spent the week before the Sturgeon Bay Open in furious preparation. He hand-tied a tapered monofilament leader heavy enough to snake Marilyn out of the rocks. He awakened his johnboat, which had been resting on its trailer behind the garage, and hosed it out. He cleaned and gapped the plugs in his old ten-horse Elgin outboard. Finally, he charged the battery that powered the johnboat's livewell and trolling motor.

On Thursday afternoon, he drove into Sturgeon Bay to pay his entry fee for the tournament.

"For an extra two bucks you can enter one of the special divisions, George," said Bump, who was serving as the tournament's grand marshal. George flipped through Bump's clipboard until he found the sheet for the senior fly-fishing division. His heart leaped. The sheet was blank! Casually, he printed his name and handed over a ten and two singles.

By Friday night, he was so intent on winning that he barely spoke to Helen. "Are you OK, George?" she asked. "You look kind of glazed over."

"Yeah, yeah. I'm focusing on the tournament tomorrow. Don't mind me. I'm focusing." He wasn't sure what focusing meant, exactly, but it was something young people did. And George's gaze returned to the little golden man on the mantel, the thin, handsome golden man who wasn't a day over thirty.

At the blastoff the next morning, Bump shouted instructions through a bullhorn and someone shot off a flare. A flotilla of bass boats churned the water to froth and disappeared in all directions. After things quieted down a bit, George backed his johnboat down the launch ramp. The Elgin started on the eleventh pull of the rope, and he motored across the bay to the far end of Sawyer Harbor.

Using the push pole, George shoved his boat into the rocky backwater that was Marilyn's lair. Standing in the bow, he put a year of wear on his right arm and shoulder as he double-hauled the big flies and heavy line. Three hours went by. The rod seemed to weigh twenty pounds. But George was still focused. He was sure Marilyn had never seen a fly, and that if he put one in front of her, she'd hit.

He wasn't counting, but it was his one hundred and third cast that finally found the right rock. The fly, a concoction of polar bear hair and marabou plumes, landed softly and floated high, wide, and handsome. From a couple of feet down, Marilyn looked it over. Slowly, she drifted up until she was almost eye to eye with it.

A puff of wind moved the fly a couple of inches. Marilyn was focused, too, and she was a fish of instant decision. She charged the fly, sucked it from the surface, and turned back to the shade and safety of her rock. But the fly didn't want to go with her. It resisted and stuck a needle into the corner of her mouth.

What was this? Outraged, Marilyn surged upward and shook her mighty head back and forth. But the fly was still there, and now it seemed to be pulling her along. Several times, she turned back toward deeper water, but the fly kept up its pressure.

Perched on the bow deck, George struggled to maintain his balance. Marilyn was too big to jump, so she slugged it out in three feet of water, charging under the boat and pulling line off the reel against the buzz of the drag. But George's rod was designed to subdue bigger fish than Marilyn, and after five minutes of battle he played her to the side of the boat. He seized her lower jaw with a thumb and forefinger and lifted her clear of the water. Then he pulled out his father's fly and admired her, his heart racing.

"Eight pounds if she's an ounce," he exulted. "Senior fly-fishing division be damned. She'll win the whole thing! She's only a pound shy of the state record!" He thought of cameras and microphones and another golden man.

He flipped the switch to pump water into the livewell. When it was full, he tried to slip Marilyn in, but she barely fit. Finally he inserted her tail-first and bent her a little. Marilyn thrashed angrily, but she settled down when the lid was closed. George picked up the push pole and began shoving the johnboat out of the shallows.

When he reached water deep enough for the outboard, he opened the livewell to check on Marilyn. One look at her started his heart racing again. She was lying on her side, and her gills were barely moving.

"Dammit," he yelled, "you can't die on me now. You've got to be alive for the weigh-in!" He turned the livewell pump back on, and left it on, to recharge the well with fresh water and oxygen. He stumbled back to the stern, choked the Elgin, and pulled the starter rope once, twice, three times, four times. The motor reeked of gasoline. It was flooded. And experience had taught George that when his Elgin got flooded, it stayed flooded. He unshipped the oars and started digging them into the water.

Unfortunately for George O'Malley, johnboats don't row very well, and neither do desperate men in their sixties. By the time he had gone a quarter mile he was winded. He dropped the oars and raised the livewell lid to check on Marilyn. All he could see was her broad, white belly. She was dying.

George grabbed her lower jaw, lifted her from the livewell, and plunged her into the water alongside the boat. He began pulling her slowly back and forth, to ease water through her gills. "Come on, come on, come on!" he begged. And then, miraculously, Marilyn's gills fluttered and she started to breathe on her own. After a few more minutes she righted herself and began to look like the old Marilyn.

George released his grip on her jaw. She hung there, a few inches below the surface, resting in the shadow of his head and shoulders.

Then she flipped her tail and swam slowly down into the cool and welcoming depths.

George felt very old and very relieved. He thought about the cameras and microphones and the little golden man. "Ahh, the hell with it," he said. His competitive fires had gone out.

No one noticed George when he arrived at the boat landing just before noon, pulled slowly along by the trolling motor and the last few amperes in the battery. The Business Boosters were busy in the circus tent they had erected for the weigh-in. In lieu of tuning up, a local garage band called the Northern Louts emitted random thumps and screeches. George backed the trailer down the ramp and loaded his boat. There was no one to talk to and not much to say, so he went home.

When he got to the lodge, Helen was drinking a Coke on the porch. "Back so soon, George?"

"Yup." He sat down heavily in a deck chair and drank half of Helen's Coke in a swallow. Then he told her about his day.

"Some fisherman I am—I caught the winner and didn't have the heart to bring her in."

"You did the right thing," said Helen. "A lot of people would have killed that fish, just to stuff it and brag about it. But not you, George. I'm proud of you."

Later that evening, while Helen and Russell dozed on a sofa by the fireplace, George carried a number of things down into the basement. Included were a brown leather tube, a canvas bag, a box of flies, a push pole—and the little golden man from the mantel.

Back upstairs, he shook Helen's shoulder gently. "Wake up so you can go to bed," he said.

Helen yawned and smiled up at him. "I know why you entered that silly tournament," she said. "It was to prove you weren't getting old, wasn't it?"

"I'll never tell."

Helen put an arm around George's waist. "Well, whatever it was, you're still my sweetheart and you're still the best-looking Irishman in Door County."

Russell grinned and wagged his tail. He had heard that one before.

Bear Trouble

///

*W*hen you're a full-grown Door County Irishman of sixty-seven winters, and you've been married for forty-five of them, there isn't much that can scare you. At that age you've learned to take most things in stride, except when you're upstairs shaving on a quiet summer morning and your wife starts screaming.

"George!" Helen shrieked. "George! Help!"

George O'Malley threw his razor into the sink and thundered down the stairs, his face still covered with foam. Helen wasn't in the dining room of Coot Lake Lodge. She wasn't in the kitchen. Frantic, George looked this way and that. Then, through one of the front windows, he saw white sneakers and slender legs wearing jeans. Helen was standing on top of the porch railing. But why, he hadn't a clue.

As George ran through the living room to the front door, he was filled with panic and wonder. Helen was a Door County Norwegian of sixty-seven summers, and not much could scare her, either. In fact, during their entire life together, George had never heard Helen scream. But she was screaming now, accompanied by Russell's furious barking. As George burst out onto the front porch, he took in the situation at a glance.

There was a bear, a large black bear, running back and forth. It was hemmed in on one side by Helen's old Buick station wagon, on the other by George's pickup, in front by Helen and the porch railing, and at the rear by Russell. Russell backed up when the bear bluffed a charge at him and advanced when it headed toward Helen, but on the average he was holding his ground.

George was surprised at Russell's courage, but he shouldn't have been. Bravery is bred in the bone of golden retrievers; among their forebears were dogs trained to leap into the sea to save drowning sailors, and apparently Russell had inherited some of the ancestral grit. But now, Russell's bravado was likely to end in big trouble. George looked around for a weapon, grabbed a broom from the porch, and ran around behind the Buick, with the idea of shooing Russell out of the way so the bear could escape.

Russell greeted George with enthusiasm. "Your turn," he seemed to say, and retreated so George could have a go. George ducked behind his pickup to give the bear a clear field, but it was suspicious. It laid its ears back and began to huff and puff and clack its teeth. George lost his patience. His wife and dog were in danger, and he, by God, was going to do something about it. A kind of madness possessed him. He ran forward, shouting, and began to beat the bear with the broom.

Bears smell bad, and they're nearsighted and not very smart, but they have feelings. And hitting a bear with a broom is an affront to its ursine dignity. This bear had had enough. It turned and lunged at George.

Time slowed down for George O'Malley. "So this is how the world ends," he thought.

And then came the last trumpet, or so it seemed to George. Actually it was Bump Olson, arriving on time for his eight o'clock appointment to pump out the lodge's septic tank. Bump had installed four air horns on the roof of his big tanker truck, and seeing George's plight, he was blowing them hard and insistently.

The bear turned to confront this new threat. Being hit with a broom was one thing, but a twelve-ton honey wagon, belching diesel smoke and bellowing like something out of Revelations, was simply too much. The bear lowered its head, dodged George, and galloped into the massive white pines that surrounded the lodge.

Bump's truck slid to a stop in a shower of gravel. George and Russell were breathing too hard to say anything. "George, would you help me down, please?" Helen asked. "It's getting to where a person can't even fill the bird feeders without being chased by a bear!"

A half hour later, the lodge's septic tank was empty and pristine. Bump joined George, Helen, and Russell on the porch for a cup of coffee and a slice of Helen's limpa bread, smeared with lingonberry jam.

"Thank God you were on time, Bump," George said. "One minute more and who knows what might have happened."

Bump grinned. "Johnny on the spot, that's my motto. But seriously, that must be the same bear that raided our garbage cans last week. Emma's afraid to let the kids play outside."

"Well, enough is enough. I'm going to call the DNR and see what they can do," said George.

Later that morning, George got Little John Hill, the local game warden, on the phone in Sturgeon Bay.

"Tell you what, George," said Little John, "we've got a culvert trap right here at the office. I'll see if I can get Leroy to bring it out and catch your bear for you."

Little John was as good as his word. About noon, he drove up in a 4x4 pickup bristling with antennas. Behind him, in another pickup pulling a trailer, was Leroy LePage, a DNR wildlife manager.

Leroy lit a dirty corncob pipe. "Ever seen a culvert trap, George? It's just a bear-sized piece of corrugated steel tube with a grating welded on one end and a sliding door on the other. We leave it right on the trailer and bait it with meat or sweet stuff, like stale bakery. The bear goes inside, and when he grabs the bait the door drops behind him and Mr. Bear is caught. Then we haul him up in the woods someplace and let him go."

"Be my guest," George said. "Need some meat?"

"Nope—brought my own." Leroy drew a large hunting knife from a sheath on his belt and cut a couple of chops off a distended, road-killed doe that was lying in the bed of his pickup. He bent down to strop the knife on the sole of his boot, but paused before returning it to its sheath.

"You want some venison, George?" Leroy asked. "There's still a couple of good roasts and a backstrap left."

"How long have you had it?"

"Well, let's see," Leroy mused. "It was lying on County Q, and I first saw it, um, must have been Tuesday, and I picked it up on Thursday, I think—so, six days, more or less. But it's been in the shade most of the time and it's just nicely mature."

George became acutely aware of the pork sausages he had eaten for breakfast. He turned away, and Helen came to his rescue.

"Thanks awfully, Leroy, but our freezer is filled right to the top," she said.

"A likely story," said Leroy. "The trouble with you, George, is that you spent too many years getting soft and picky down in Chicago. We've got to toughen you up. But first things first. That bear probably was after the suet in your bird feeders, so I'll park the trap next to 'em. It'll catch retrievers too, so keep your dog away and call me as soon as you see the door is down."

When Little John and Leroy had left, peace descended on the lodge. Helen smiled warmly at George and gave him a kiss. "Sweetheart, that was a brave thing you did, going after that bear with nothing more than a broom."

"A mere bagatelle," George said, expansive in victory. "Bears are just big clowns. I wasn't any braver than Russell, and if worse came to worst I could have run for it. There's no bear alive that can outrun me!"

But George found it hard to sleep that night. The odor of bear was still in his nose, and every creak of the lodge's ancient rafters and joists sounded like a big animal coming up the stairs. Finally, about three thirty, he heard a distinct clunk that had promise. He got out of bed and took a look. The trailer was rocking in the moonlight and the door was closed. They had caught Mr. Bear.

Leroy arrived after breakfast the next morning. George, Helen, and Russell looked into the trap as he hitched up the trailer.

"Well, he's got excellent teeth," George said, with a shudder. "It's been fun, but the farther away you haul him the better I'll like it."

Leroy knocked out his corncob on the heel of his boot. "I have a spot all picked out about 150 miles from here. But hey, George, have you got a camera I can borrow? Mine's on the fritz, and I'd like to take some pictures of this bear when I release it."

"You bet," George said. In a minute he was back outside with the faithful Nikon F2 he had bought in the seventies. "It's a real camera, not a digital, and there's a twenty-four-exposure roll of film in it. The exposure is set to 'sunny sixteen,' it's focused halfway out, and the motor drive will shoot three frames a second. Just point it at the bear and hold the shutter down. It'll keep going until it runs out of film."

Three hours later, in the heart of northern Oconto County, Leroy stopped at the intersection of two sand roads in an old clearing that was growing up in scrub oak and sweet fern. He climbed on top of the trap, turned on the camera, and raised the door. The bear exploded from the trap in a black blur and headed for the nearest big trees.

When Leroy came back to the lodge with the camera, George removed the film. "I've got to go to Sturgeon Bay this afternoon anyway, so I'll go to the two-hour processing place and get prints made, and then I'll drop them off at your office."

"OK," said Leroy. "There might be a couple of good ones, but it all happened real fast. It was about a hundred yards from the trap to the woods, and I think that bear set a new record. You know, people think bears can't move, but they've been clocked at thirty miles an hour."

George smiled politely at Leroy. Thirty miles an hour! He visualized a foot race between an Olympic sprinter and a lumbering black bear. No way.

When George picked up the prints he sat down behind the wheel of his pickup and looked at them. Leroy had shot the entire roll. Print number one showed the bear just coming out of the trap, and on print twenty-four it was disappearing into the trees.

George began to sweat a bit. Twenty-four frames at three frames per second meant the bear had done a standing hundred-yard dash in eight seconds.

George's sweat turned cold. "And only yesterday morning, I was hitting that bugger in the butt with a broom and bragging that I could outrun him," he groaned. What was worse, he had wasted a chance to pull slightly ahead in the never-ending give and take of married life with Helen.

"Stupid me," he thought. "She told me I was brave, and I blew it off. Now when I find out how brave I really was, it's too late to take advantage of it!"

George had the hollow feeling that follows a missed shot at a deer or a big fish lost at the side of the boat. "If I had any brains, I could have parlayed that bear into a new outboard motor," he muttered.

Back at the lodge that night, the old Seth Thomas clock on the mantel bonged eleven times. George stuck a bookmark in *Barchester Towers* and tapped the ashes out of his pipe.

Helen and Russell were dozing on the sofa in front of the fireplace. George shook Helen's shoulder gently. "Wake up so you can go to bed."

As they headed upstairs together, Helen was playful. She grabbed George's backside. "I'm a big bad bear and I'm gonna getcha!"

"Not tonight," George said. He wasn't in the mood.

The Baileys Harbor Bird and Booyah Club

///

*G*eorge tucked the butt of his rifle firmly into his shoulder and centered the crosshairs of its scope on a target tacked up a hundred yards away. A ribbon tied to a stake near the target was fluttering slightly to the left in the April breeze, so he shifted his point of aim an inch to the right to compensate for wind drift.

He carefully touched the trigger with his fingertip, took a deep breath, blew it out, took a shallow breath, held it, and started his trigger squeeze, concentrating on his finger and gradually increasing its pressure until . . .

Someone behind him spoke.

"Hey, have you seen a little brown dog?"

George took his finger off the trigger and ejected the unfired .22 cartridge onto his shooting bench. He turned and saw a rotund middle-aged man, with a full white beard and mustache, standing a few feet away. "Who the hell is this?" George wondered. "Hemingway or Santa Claus?"

"Sorry if I startled you. My name is Hans Berge. Actually, as of today I'm your neighbor—my wife and I are moving into the old brick farmhouse down the road.

"Anyway, I was walking my dog and a few minutes ago he took off after a rabbit. He's a city dog and it was probably the first rabbit he ever saw. Now he's disappeared, and if anything happens to him my wife will kill me."

"Well, we can't have that," George said. "I'll help you look. By the way, my name is . . ."

"George, look what I've got!"

Helen was walking up the path from the lodge to George's shooting range on the hillside, carrying a thermos and a paper bag. A shaggy terrier was running in front of her, followed by Russell, who was walking sedately at heel.

"Ollie!" said Hans. "There you are!" The terrier sprinted the last few yards and jumped up into his arms.

Helen laughed. "Well, there's no doubt about who he belongs to. What a little charmer!"

"Yes, isn't he? We call him Ollie because when we feed him he always looks up and makes big puppy eyes, like Oliver Twist. You know—'Please, sir, I want some more.'"

"If you're our new neighbor," Helen said, "I just met your wife down at the mailboxes. My name is Helen O'Malley, and I assume you've already met my husband, George?"

"Informally." He put Ollie on the ground for Russell to sniff and shook hands with Helen and George.

"I'll bet Ollie would like a sticky bun," said Helen, "right out of the oven. And you, too, Mr. Berge, please sit down and have a bun and some coffee."

Berge dragged a rusty folding chair to a corner of the shooting bench, as far as he could get from George's rifle. "Just one, and call me Hans," he said. "Actually Ollie is on a diet, and so am I. Living in Chicago, we were both pretty sedentary, and now that I own a little piece of countryside, Beth—that's my wife—commands that we take a one-hour walk every day."

"Well, feel free to walk on our land," Helen offered, "and bring Ollie. Russell is an only dog, and the two of them can swim in the lake."

She removed the cap from the thermos and poured coffee into the plastic cups that nested within it. They talked about dogs and Door County and what they had done for a living in Chicago.

George and Helen were taken aback to learn that Berge had been a psychiatrist—the only Norwegian shrink in Chicago, he said—with an office in the Loop, across the river from George's copy desk at the *Sun-Times*.

"I could have practiced for a few more years, but I decided to retire when my patients started playing with their phones during sessions. Believe it or not, they would lie there on the couch and send text messages when they were supposed to be free-associating."

"Now I'm in trouble," George said. "I might not hold up under analysis."

"Don't worry, I have a code of ethics: I don't start analyzing until you start paying. But tell me, George, what were you shooting at before I interrupted?"

"A hundred-meter .22 rimfire target. I use the clay bank over there as a backstop. Actually it's only a hundred yards, but a hundred meters makes it sound harder."

"You mean you can hit something at that distance with a .22?"

"You bet. This is a Winchester Model 52, the best American target rifle ever made. I've had it for forty years and it's just getting broken in. Shooting from a bench like this it will put ten shots into an inch on a good day, if you use match ammo. Here, give it a try."

He picked up the rifle and held it out, but Berge edged away. "Maybe some other time," he said, and looked at his watch. "It's been nice talking to you, and thanks for the coffee and the bun, but Beth will be wondering where we are. Come on, Ollie."

When Hans and his dog had disappeared over the hill, George slung his rifle and gave Helen a kiss tasting of black coffee and cinnamon.

"What did you think of our new neighbor?" she asked.

"Well, he adds a touch of class to Coot Lake Road," George said as they started down the path to the lodge. "Very distinguished. Sure is gun-shy, though—I suppose he disapproves of people who shoot."

As April turned into May, Hans and George met a couple of times a week when Hans's rambles brought him near the lodge, and Helen and Beth met almost every day when they went out to the road for the mail. Being men, Hans and George never talked about anything personal, and being women, Helen and Beth rarely talked about anything else.

"Well, I think I know why Hans was leery of your rifle," Helen commented after breakfast one morning. "When we first met, Hans said he was a psychiatrist, but he didn't say what kind. Yesterday, Beth told me he was a Freudian of the old school. And to a Freudian, she says, a gun is a—well, it's a symbol."

"A symbol of what?"

"Never mind, George, it would just make you angry."

"Oh, I get it," George said. "Ye gods, how do people come up with such goofy ideas?"

On the first Saturday in May, Hans and Beth threw a house-warming party and invited George and Helen and Bump and Emma. After supper, the men retired to the front porch to watch the sunset and finish off a bottle of local cherry wine. George had brought his binoculars and was looking at birds in the yard.

"That one on the ground over there is a white-crowned sparrow, and the two behind it are white-throated sparrows. The warblers usually come through right after the sparrows, so the main migration can't be more than a few days off. Some day next week we'll wake up in the morning and there will be warblers everywhere, like little flying flowers."

"George, that was poetic," said Hans. "I wouldn't know a warbler if I saw one, and I didn't know there were different kinds of sparrows. But how can you shoot a rifle one day and watch birds the next? It seems like a contradiction."

"Well, it's not," Bump said. "Take me, for instance. I pump poop for a living, and I hunt and fish practically year-round, but I'm also a past president of the Baileys Harbor Bird and Booyah Club. Some days I enjoy nature with binoculars, some days with a knife and fork."

"What's the Baileys Harbor Bird and Booyah Club?" Hans asked.

"It's just George and me and Doug Caldwell, the deputy sheriff, and Leroy LePage, the wildlife manager, and George's buddy Jack Paisley. We meet one Saturday a month at Snuffy's Tavern. Dues are a round of Guinness. If there are birds around we watch 'em, and if not we go fishing or shoot George's .22.

"As for booyah, that's a kind of Belgian chicken stew. You take a couple of chickens and toss 'em in a big kettle with whatever vegetables you got handy—potatoes, carrots, cabbage, tomatoes, turnips, rutabagas, onions. You put in a bottle of Wooster sauce and a couple of lemons and a handful of salt and cook it outdoors for about twelve hours, and then you skim off the surplus feathers, eat a little, and freeze the rest."

"You're more than welcome to join the club," offered George. "Don't let the booyah scare you—we only make it once a year, and you don't have to eat it if you don't want to."

"Count me in," Hans said. "You guys were lucky—you learned about the outdoors when you were still boys. But as a kid in Chicago, I missed out on all that. The only wild animals I ever saw were the Cubs and the Bears.

"And then, after I went into practice, I would sit in my office in the Loop, looking out of a dirty window at pigeons on the sill, and listen to housewives from Lake Forest complain about their husbands. And all the time I was thinking of hawks, not pigeons, and wishing I could walk in a real forest. I know it sounds silly, but I've always wanted to be a serious birdwatcher, and now it's probably too late."

"No, it's never too late," George said, "and it certainly isn't silly. You just need experience. I can give you a crash course on the local birds, starting tomorrow, and before you know it you'll be initiated. Meet me about five in the morning and we'll take a walk around the lake. You can borrow Helen's binoculars."

Hans showed up on time and learned fast. He could spot the slightest movement, and he rarely had to be shown a bird twice.

"You're a hellish quick study, Hans," George said, after they had been birding together for a week. "You've been keeping a list—how many warblers have you seen?"

"According to the book, there are about thirty-two species you might see in Door County, and so far I've found twenty-nine of them—all but the Louisiana Waterthrush, the Prothonotary, and the Cerulean. But I suppose you've seen them all, George."

"Except for one. I've never seen a Cerulean, after all these years. It's my jinx bird. Once I was standing right next to Bump when he saw one. He told me where to look, and I still didn't see it."

As the second week of the migration went by, Hans began birding on his own, prowling through The Ridges Sanctuary and the state parks with the Zeiss binoculars he had ordered from New York. On Wednesday afternoon he met George on the shore of Coot Lake.

"We're tied, George," he said. "I didn't see the Waterthrush, but I heard it pretty clearly, and I saw a female Prothonotary along Logan Creek. So now we're both looking for a Cerulean."

"Lots of luck, Hans. The migration is almost over and the Ceruleans get scarcer every year. It'll take a really lucky birder to see one now."

One morning, Helen met Beth at the mailboxes. "Is George overdoing it?" she asked. "Does Hans really like all this birding, or is he just going along with it to be polite?"

"He's having the time of his life," said Beth. "He's walked off seven pounds so far, and I've never seen him so interested in anything. He really likes the warblers because they just fly around and sing and don't have any complexes or neuroses."

George spent the third week of May in Chicago, helping Bill and Josie with some painting and varnishing. "Anything new in the neighborhood, Helen?" he asked when he got back.

"A lot. Hans has something to show you, but I won't spoil the story. You should get it from him firsthand."

"If he saw a Cerulean, I'll murder him," George said.

After breakfast the next morning, George walked down the road to Hans and Beth's old farmhouse. He was surprised to see Bump's camping tent pitched in their backyard.

"What's with the tent, Hans?"

"Well, you had better sit down, George. This is going to take a while.

"The day after you left, Ollie and I went over to your place about four in the morning to bird from the pier. I saw something move way up at the top of that big box elder on the south shore—a little bird with a white belly and a blue back and a necklace—and I thought, by God, it's a Cerulean warbler. I walked to the end of the pier to get a better look, and Ollie started yapping. I turned around and dammit, there was a skunk about halfway out the pier, and Ollie was on the shore barking at it.

"Well, to make a long story short, the skunk sprayed me, and then Ollie chased it up the hillside toward the lodge. Helen was on the porch and I thought of asking her to lend me your rifle, but I didn't even know how to load it. So I looked around for something to throw, but I was too late."

"Oh, no!"

"Oh, yes," Hans groaned. "It must have been a double-barreled skunk, because he got Ollie dead center. I mean, the poor dog was dripping. I figured the skunk had already done his worst, so I picked Ollie up by the scruff and threw him in the lake, and then I jumped in after him, but apparently skunk stink isn't water soluble.

"So I took him home and we both scrubbed up with tomato juice, but all that did was turn us orange. Then I found a formula on the Internet—hydrogen peroxide, baking soda, and liquid soap—but we had to drive into town to get the peroxide, and by the time we got the stuff mixed up the smell had kind of set in Ollie's fur, and in my beard, too.

"Well, there was no way Ollie was going to sleep on our bed smelling like he did, so I got out his dog crate, with the idea that he could sleep in it on the back porch until he was deodorized.

"But Beth felt sorry for him—you know, the poor little dog out there all by himself—and she said I didn't smell too great, either. So I borrowed Bump's tent, and Ollie and I have been sleeping in it for a week.

"So here's my question, George. It's been seven nights in the tent. Ollie and I are almost back to normal, and I've seen all the warblers I'm going to see this year. Do you think I qualify as a member of the Baileys Harbor Bird and Booyah Club?"

"Yeah, I think you've had your initiation," said George. "You got skunk spray in your beard and saw a Cerulean warbler on the same day. That's about as good as it gets, and the club welcomes you with open arms—metaphorically, that is. We aren't big on hugs."

"Neither am I," Hans said. "And now I've got something to show you." He went into the house and returned with two bottles of Guinness and a shiny new Savage .22 target rifle topped with a long and expensive scope. "What do you think, George? I had to drive all the way to Oshkosh to get it."

"It's a beauty, Hans, but what would Freud think? I thought a rifle was supposed to be, you know, a symbol."

"It's only a theory, George," Hans replied. He lit a Montecristo Churchill and blew out a cloud of smoke. "Cigars are supposed to be symbols, too, but Freud said that sometimes a cigar is only a cigar. Well, sometimes a rifle is only a rifle. Freud might not approve, but what did he know? There weren't any skunks in downtown Vienna.

"George, I'd like you to teach me how to shoot this rifle—today, if possible. I used to be gun-shy, but I've learned my lesson. If that skunk shows up again, he'll get one warning shot, and after that it's him or me."

The Hound
of the Basketballs

///

*A*s the last bright leaves of autumn fade and fall, the tourist trade in Door County fades with them. A few of the restaurants, boutiques, and gift shops stay open on late fall weekends, but most are closed for the season, and it gets hard to find designer jeans, gourmet jelly beans, or a copy of the *Wall Street Journal*.

When the summer rush is over, the county seems deserted, but George and Helen and the rest of the year-round residents are still there. They take advantage of the last few warm days to work outdoors and enjoy a freedom that has been denied them since May: when they go into town they can park almost anywhere, even in Sister Bay.

As winter approaches, the peninsula becomes a stretched-out small town, with most of a small town's virtues and vices. Out in the country, men bolt snowplow blades on their pickup trucks and keep their neighbors' driveways open. Women with SUVs pick up other women and go shopping together when the weather looks bad. Like small-town people everywhere, they go to great lengths to be helpful, but when they have nothing better to do, they talk about each other. And when facts are scarce, they are not averse to speculation.

The people who live on Coot Lake Road constitute a friendly little community. They don't talk about each other very much because they already know most of what there is to know. Help is there for the asking: Helen and her old Buick station wagon offer a free taxi service when only a really big car will do, and George is available as an all-around handyman. Bump plows snow, Emma does everyone's taxes, Hans offers sage counsel, and Beth dusts off her nursing degree when colds and the flu are making the rounds.

And then there's Lloyd Barnes. These days he serves as director of security for the Coot Lake neighborhood, keeping an eye on strange cars that wander down their dead-end road. But last October, when he moved in, he was just a name on a mailbox, a man of mystery and unusual habits who lived alone in a cottage across the road from Hans and Beth. He left after sundown most nights and returned before daybreak, driving an old Ford pickup with out-of-state plates, and always in the company of a big yellow dog. He spoke to no one and was glimpsed only once or twice in the daylight. A dense stand of white cedar trees hid his cottage from view, and within a week or two of his arrival, he was out of mind and largely forgotten.

Largely, but not by Helen. Driving home from a bridge game one night, she turned onto Fairview Road and saw him in the headlights for a few seconds, a tall, lean figure walking on the shoulder, with his dog ranging ahead on a long leash. Her heart immediately went out to him.

"Where's he been and where's he going," she wondered, "walking his dog down a back road at midnight, miles from home? There's more to him than meets the eye."

She later tried to tempt Lloyd by inviting him for pie and coffee on a Saturday afternoon, and when she found that he had an unlisted telephone number, she left a handwritten invitation in his mailbox at the foot of the driveway. But he didn't come for pie and coffee.

"I'm going to check on him tomorrow, George," Helen said. "I want to make sure he's all right."

"Helen, I've barely laid eyes on the man, and we have no business pestering him. Maybe he works nights. Maybe he just doesn't like people, or he's dodging a bill collector or some woman's angry husband. In any case, if he wants to be a hermit, it's no skin off our nose."

Helen agreed, but she kept an eye peeled just the same. October passed, and Barnes was still an enigma. In November, Helen recruited Beth as a spy.

"From your porch, you should be able to look down his driveway with Hans's sixty-power birding scope," said Helen. "Give me a call if you see anything."

Beth rang back just before dark. "Helen!" she said, breathless with excitement. "I just got a really good sighting on the first try. He was getting in his truck with his dog. With that scope I could count the buttons on his jacket, and is he a hunk! About six two, big blue eyes, and he looks like Paul Newman!"

Helen's concern for the furtive Mr. Barnes redoubled. She told George about Beth's sighting.

"George, why would a man who looks like Paul Newman live alone with only a hound dog for company?" she asked.

"I dunno. Maybe he's been married once already and learned his lesson."

"Very funny."

"Yes, I thought it was one of my better ones," George said.

Thanksgiving was early that year, on the twenty-first of the month, and on the morning of the twentieth George went to the barbershop in Baileys Harbor for a trim and a chance to catch up on the local news. He found that the barber and the waiting customers were talking about his secretive neighbor.

"Hey, George, that Barnes guy lives just down the road from you. What do you know about him?" the barber asked.

"Nothing. I've never met him or even had a close look at him. He keeps to himself."

"Well, I wish that dog of his would do the same," said a shaky eighty-year-old with a Brewers cap. "I was just dropping off to sleep one night in October when it came howling into my backyard and chased a coon up a cherry tree. I went out in my pj's to run it off, and the goddam thing came right up on the porch. It was all I could do to get in the back door before it took a chunk out of me."

"I've seen it too," said Huey Sikorsky, a rural mail carrier from Northport. "Effie, she don't want me to smoke in the house, so I was out on the driveway about midnight the week before last, and Barnes come by hell-bent for election in his pickup, with that dog hangin' out the window and goin' *aroop-aroop* like the hound of the basketballs or whatever. Scared the crap outta me!

"And you know Heine Lipschultz? He practically lives in Snuffy's Tavern, and he says Barnes has been meeting Doug Caldwell and Little John in Snuffy's parking lot at night. Heine was sitting in his car kind of sleeping it off, and he saw Deputy Doug give Barnes a pair of binoculars and one of them big spotlights that plugs into the cigarette lighter, and Little John gave him a cell phone and some other gadget, maybe a GPS. Now what do you make of that?"

"I haven't got a clue, Huey," George said. "You'll have to ask Doug."

Driving home, George turned the Lloyd Barnes puzzle over in his mind.

"What a bunch of busybodies we all are! Like a flock of chickens pecking at the odd one. But still—the guy meets a deputy sheriff and a warden in a parking lot and gets a bunch of electronic toys. Looks like he's investigating something, but what, or whom? And why is the dog involved?"

When George got back to the lodge, he told Helen what he had heard. Then he gave up minding his own business and called Deputy Doug.

"Hey, Doug, this is George. I'll come right to the point. What can you tell me about Lloyd Barnes?"

"Nothing, George. At least not right now. Just stay out of his way. He's a busy man."

Helen had been thinking about Barnes practically nonstop, and after lunch, she made up her mind.

"Enough is enough, George. Who's he watching—us? It's time we found out what's going on. Why don't we invite him to

Thanksgiving dinner tomorrow and see if he'll open up a little after a good meal."

"I suppose it wouldn't hurt to try," George said. "But don't be surprised if he tells us to take a running jump."

Later that afternoon, George and Helen drove up Barnes's driveway and tapped at his door. From the porch they saw a window curtain move, and then the door opened partway. They could hear a dog sniffing deeply and whining to get out.

"Kin ah hep yew?" Barnes asked. "Excuse me for not openin' the door all the way, but if I did y'all would have a hundred pounds of hound kissin' you half to death."

George and Helen glanced at each other. They hadn't expected a southern accent.

"Mr. Barnes," said Helen, "I'm Helen O'Malley and this is my husband, George."

"Yes, I know who y'all are."

"It's kind of late notice, but all of us who live on Coot Lake Road are having a potluck Thanksgiving dinner at our place. We want you to join us and we won't take no for an answer."

"You're layin' down the law, are you, ma'am? Well, I don't have anything to bring, or anything decent to wear, either."

"Doesn't matter, Mr. Barnes," responded Helen. "You can bring something next time."

"And we aren't dressing up," added George. "No ties allowed. We'll eat at two, and we'd love to have you—and your dog, too."

"Well, I'll have to give that some thought. He's kind of overwhelming. But I'll be there, and thanks for the invite."

Back at the lodge, George gave Helen a high five. "You did it!" he said. "You finally got him to come out of his shell."

"Yes, I did, George. I've been trying to invade his privacy for six weeks, and now that I have, I feel guilty about it. Well, let's see what tomorrow brings."

On Thanksgiving Day, the Coot Lake gang gathered at the lodge. Two o'clock came and went, but there was no sign of Barnes.

"Well, maybe we didn't penetrate the shell after all," George said. "But at least we tried. Let's eat."

Then Russell heard an unfamiliar engine and ran to the door. Barnes drove up, ten minutes late, but rugged and muscular in the green and khaki uniform of the Tennessee Highway Patrol, complete with a flat-brimmed campaign hat. He opened the passenger door of his pickup and released a large and lugubrious yellow hound with long, droopy ears and a wrinkled forehead.

George went outside to greet him. "Sorry if I kept you waiting, but I was finishing up some paperwork at the courthouse," said Barnes. "This here is Grits. Hope you don't mind if he weedles on one of y'all's trees—he's been cooped up in the truck for hours. I call him Grits because he's the color of hominy and melted butter."

Thanksgiving dinner was on the table, and they ate turkey, sage and onion dressing, cranberry sauce, mashed potatoes, and rutabaga. Flustered by the handsome stranger they had wondered about for weeks, the women hovered around, admiring his uniform and offering him seconds and thirds. Then they all watched a football game and polished off three pies and two pots of coffee. When the game was over, Russell, Ollie, Grits, and the Olson kids went outside to play under the yard lights, and the adults adjourned to the sofas in front of the fireplace. George poured glasses of Carlsville cherry wine for everyone.

"It was good to be here today," Lloyd said. "I wasn't looking forward to having Thanksgiving dinner in a restaurant."

"That's what neighbors are for," replied George. "Frankly, we've been worrying about you, mostly because we can't figure out what you're doing. We're all being busybodies, I guess, but we mean well."

Lloyd grinned at them. "Y'all are forgiven. And I guess it's safe to tell you the tale now.

"I was a Tennessee state trooper for twenty-five years, and when I hung it up a couple of years ago I started working for my cousin Lonnie—he breeds bloodhounds and coonhounds and bear hounds. That's how I come by Grits. Lonnie figures Grits's pa was an English coonhound that clumb the fence and had his way with a bloodhound bitch that was in season. One of the pups from that litter was this funny yellow color, and Lonnie gave him to me. Turns out that Grits inherited the best of both. He runs like a coonhound, and his nose is about as powerful as the Hubble telescope.

"Back in late September Lonnie had me deliver three Plott hounds to a customer in Green Bay. I drove up here to have a look around, and I liked the place so much I decided to stay. Don't tell anybody from Tennessee I said this, but after all those years I got sick of the heat and a steady diet of catfish and barbecue. Anyway, the day after I moved in I paid a courtesy call on the sheriff here, and he asked me if I wanted a little part-time night work as a deputy. He said he and the DNR were trying to catch some lowlifes that knew every cop and warden in the county by sight, and he wondered if an undercover man could round 'em up before they found out who he was."

"Aha!" George said. "I thought as much. You and Grits were sniffing for drug dealers."

"No, George, it was a lot smellier than that. We were after illegal poop. Turns out the lowlifes bought an old tanker truck and they were pumping septic tanks and holding tanks at night, real cheap. But instead of taking the stuff to the sewage treatment plant and paying to get rid of it, they would dump it in swamps, old orchards, even in the roadside ditches—a little here, a little there. There was no shortage of evidence—the problem was finding the source.

"So ol' Grits and I became a two-man all-night sanitary squad. We kept out of sight during the day and drove around after dark with our eyes and noses open. At first I walked Grits on the roadsides, but after a while I realized we could cover a lot more country in the truck with the window open.

"Once he got the idea, Grits would find the stuff, and with that chokebore nose he could backtrack the pumper truck. I mean, any ol' dog can smell shit, but Grits is an expert . . . He can single out individual batches and tell you where they came from. Anyway, we caught both of the perps last week. Y'all can read about it in the papers in a few days."

"One more question," said George. "Did Grits ever chase a raccoon into somebody's backyard?'

"Oh, you heard about that? Yeah, that was priceless. Back when we were still walkin' at night, a coon crossed the road in front of us and Grits took off after it and pulled the leash right out of my hand. He took the coon into a backyard and it clumb up a little cherry tree. Grits was barkin', and the coon was bouncin' up and down and hangin' on for dear life.

"So, this old guy come out in his nightshirt with a softball bat and started bellerin', 'Here now! Here now!' Well, ol' Grits is the soul of good nature and he figured the guy was callin' him for supper, so he went on the back porch and the old boy slammed the door so hard he broke the glass.

"But what I'm waitin' on is the trial. Grits is on the prosecution witness list as G. Barnes—just a little cop joke—and it'll be interesting to watch the defense attorney's face at the preliminary hearing when he finds out G. Barnes has four legs and a tail.

"Anyway that's why I haven't been a very good neighbor. But now we're closed for the winter, I'm off the night shift, and Grits and I are really going to retire."

"Good," George said. "Tell me, Lloyd, do you like birds?"

"You bet. They're my favorite dish."

"I mean just looking at them."

"I always look at 'em right before I eat 'em," Lloyd replied, and laughed. "I know what you're getting at, George. The big fella with the beard told me all about your club and I joined up an hour ago.

"There is one problem, though—can a lapsed Baptist drink Guinness?"

"Just think of it as liquid bread," said George.

Lloyd was the last to leave. "Thank you, Helen," he said. "I haven't had a Thanksgiving dinner like this since I was a boy. You're my favorite busybody. And please tell Beth she won't have to look at me with that spotting scope anymore. She can drop in anytime."

When Lloyd had left, George poured himself another glass of wine.

"Well, my little chickadee, it just goes to show you—about the time you think you have somebody pegged, he turns out to be something else. I thought he was a deadbeat, and in fact he was a cop. A lesson to us all."

"Yes, and isn't he handsome in his uniform?" Helen asked.

"That's not my department."

"Well, take it from me, he is. And on top of that he's sort of exotic and dangerous until you get to know him. Drop-dead attractive, in other words. Now that he will be out in the daylight, every unattached middle-aged female north of Sturgeon Bay will be after him, and his troubles are just beginning."

"Would you like me to be exotic?"

"No, George, I like you the way you are. At my time of life I prefer a known quantity."

"I suppose," George said. "Not to change the subject, but is there any of your cherry pie left?"

"You bet. I was keeping an eye on it, and when there were only two pieces left I slipped it into the icebox. There's some turkey, too—do you want a sandwich?"

"Helen, you read my mind. White meat, please, on rye, and heavy on the mayonnaise."

When they finished their snack it was bedtime, and they climbed the stairs together. George put his arm around Helen's shoulders. "I've got to hand it to you, kiddo—you make the best pie crust I ever ate—flaky, tasty, sweet, and light. I tried a little sliver of Emma's pecan pie, and compared to yours, her crust was like old linoleum."

Helen cocked her head on one side and gave George a look. "And what is all this soft soap supposed to accomplish?"

"It's funny," said George. "Turkey usually makes me sleepy, but not tonight. I'm wide awake and dangerous."

"George T. O'Malley," Helen said. "You've always got an excuse."

The Outcasts
of Caribou Camp

Supper was over, and George and Helen were doing the dishes when the phone on the kitchen counter rang. George pushed the speaker button, and a loud and familiar voice boomed into the room.

"Hey, Georgie, how the hell are ya?"

George turned to Helen and rolled his eyes. "I believe it's Cousin Patrick."

"Either him or the foghorn," Helen whispered.

"So how's it goin'? You hangin' in there, Georgie?" Patrick bellowed. "Uncle Theron and I need a favor from you, if you're up to it."

"You know I hate it when you call me Georgie, and I can hear you fine, Pat, you don't have to shout. What do you want?"

"Well, Georgie, you remember Caribou Camp, don't ya, that place up in Ontario where Theron and I used to catch the big lake trout? Well, we're going there again, but it's eight hundred miles one way from Chicago, maybe more. I can do my share of the driving but Theron will be eighty pretty soon, and he's getting a little unsteady behind the wheel.

"So that's where you come in, Georgie. I need you to help me drive and do some of the chores. You'll love it; there's terrific fishing right in front of the cabin. And it'll be a break for Helen, too. Are you listening, Helen? C'mon, won't it be great to get rid of Georgie for a week?"

Helen raised her hands in surrender. "You'd better go along, George. I have a feeling I'm not going to win this one."

Patrick let out a whoop of victory. "Did you hear that, Theron? Helen says Georgie can come with us! I tell ya, she's the best thing that ever happened to him. Theron, come over here and talk to Helen for a while."

Theron picked up the phone. A lifelong bachelor and a retired professor of English from the University of Chicago, he shared an apartment near Jackson Park with his noisy nephew, Patrick Moore.

"Thanks for letting George come with us, Helen," said Theron. "It's a lot to ask, but Pat and I wanted to go fishing in Canada one more time, and we aren't getting any younger. And Pat is right when he says you're the best thing that ever happened to George. I just wish I had seen you first."

Helen smiled at George, who was filling his pipe. "I'm flattered, Theron, but you're ten years older than me, and always have been."

"Yes, of course. And yet . . ."

"All right, break it up, you lovebirds," Patrick said. "Helen, I need a favor from you, too. Could you buy enough food for three men for a week? And figure out a menu? Just simple stuff that Georgie can cook. Keep your receipts and we'll settle up when we get there, OK?"

"OK, Pat. When will that be?"

"We'll see you about suppertime on Thursday."

"Thursday!" George barked. "You mean this coming Thursday? Dammit, Pat, today is Tuesday already!"

"Yeah, I know, it's kind of short notice, but I figured that if I waited until the last minute, you couldn't refuse. We'll have to leave early Friday morning because our reservation for the cabin starts Saturday at noon. All right? See you then, Georgie, and Theron says good-bye."

When the line went dead, George poured himself a cup of coffee, sat down at the kitchen table, and shook his head in disbelief.

"God, what an operator—slick as the floor in a butcher shop. You can tell he's been a used car salesman all his life. But you didn't put up much of a fight, Helen."

Helen sighed. "I didn't have the heart to. Patrick makes a lot of racket, but he doesn't fool me. He's been awfully lonely since Martha died. And Theron has been at loose ends ever since he retired. They're getting old, George, and they haven't got anyone to look after them except Bill and Josie and you and me. And it's our turn. How could I say no?"

"What a girl," George thought, for about the thousandth time in his married life. "Am I lucky or what?"

Friday morning Helen served a big breakfast: sausages, pancakes with brown puddles of Rollie Jorns's maple syrup, and biscuits made from scratch. Then the men piled into a big German sedan Patrick had driven up from Chicago. George got behind the wheel and looked out over the expanse of its hood.

"A classic Door County car—a black BMW with Illinois plates. Did you buy this thing from yourself?"

Patrick winked at George. "You bet! I always wanted one of these Beemers, so I gave myself a helluva deal and only took a 10 percent commission. I'll sell it back to the business when this trip is over."

And off they went, down the Door Peninsula to Green Bay, and then west across Wisconsin and north through Minnesota to a motel at International Falls. They crossed the border into Ontario the next morning, and Patrick stopped at a store that was just opening. He was back in a few minutes, staggering beneath the weight of three cases of Bullmoose Ale and two boxes of Havana cigars. "Welcome to Canada," he said, as he opened a Bullmoose and lit a panatela. "You drive, Georgie, and I'll navigate."

Three hours later Patrick told George to slow down. "I'm pretty sure that's their road just ahead. When I called in April, the manager said they had been all filled up, but there was a cancellation, so I grabbed it. I didn't catch all he had to say because I was talking to a customer and filling out a finance contract at the same time."

The roadside sign looked brand new. Caribou Camp, it read, and then in smaller letters, "Federated Scottish Reformed Church of Canada." George slammed on the brakes. "Pat, you've booked us into a church camp! You'd better have another beer—if this is a strict church it might be your last one for a week."

"Oh, for God's sake," said Patrick. "I guess the place has changed hands since we were here last. That must have been what the guy was trying to tell me on the phone. Well, what the hell—we're here, and I've already paid, so let's make the best of it."

Caribou Camp was a row of housekeeping cabins facing a sheltered bay. Each cabin had a Canadian-style sloping boat ramp, a wooden rowboat, and an outhouse set back in the woods. At the center of the waterfront was a bonfire ring surrounded by benches. When George, Patrick, and Theron got out of the car they were greeted by a tall, smiling man with red hair, a clerical collar, and a businesslike manner.

"Hello, hello," he said. "I'm Duncan Ross, the manager, and you must be our guests from the States, eh? You're lucky we had a cancellation, because all the other resorts on the lake are full. Your cabin is number seven, right over there. Would you like some help unloading your car?"

George glanced at the cases of Bullmoose on the back seat. "No, no, thank you, that won't be necessary. We can manage fine. Just fine."

"We lead a quiet life at Caribou Camp," explained Ross. "A little fishing, a little contemplation, and a lot of inner peace. Every evening we gather for Bible study here at the fire ring, and of course you're welcome to join us and share your favorite passages."

"Certainly, Reverend," Patrick replied. "I'm particularly fond of the wedding at Cana, where water was turned into wine. And without any grapes, believe it or not. My grandfather used to make wine in the bathtub, but he always needed grapes."

"Yes. I see. I'm familiar with the story—of Cana, that is, not your grandfather. Perhaps there will be time to work it in."

When Ross was out of earshot, George berated Patrick in an

angry whisper. "Now you've done it, Pat! They don't need three infidels like us around here. Let's get while the getting is good."

"And go where, George?" Patrick asked. "Back to Chicago? You heard the man, everything is full up. So we have to act churchy for a week. We did it when we were kids. How hard can it be?"

In a larger cabin that served as the Caribou Camp headquarters, Duncan Ross poured his wife a cup of tea.

"You know, Agatha, it's my job to keep these cabins full all summer, but I wonder if I should have booked those Yanks. The tall one makes fun of miracles, the middle-sized one seems awfully nervous about something, and the older one doesn't say anything at all."

"Well, let's not worry about them yet, not when we have real trouble at our doorstep," cautioned Agatha. "Duncan, we really have to do something about the MacGregor twins in cabin eight. They're sixteen and quite mature young women already, and frankly, they're chasing everything remotely male—even Pastor Ferguson, and you know what he's like. And those microscopic bathing suits they wear are a scandal."

"Are they? I hadn't noticed."

"Oh, yes, you have. Every man between Montreal and Medicine Hat has noticed those girls. And vice versa."

After a breakfast of Spam and eggs the next morning, George, Patrick, and Theron walked down to the shore to have a look at their boat. Reverend Ross joined them.

"If it's lake trout you're after, this is all you need," he said, and handed George a heavy trolling rod with a big silver wobbling spoon dangling from its tip. "There's a hundred feet of water just a stone's throw offshore. Let out line until you hit bottom, and then row back and forth in front of the cabins and jig the spoon up and down. But be careful—these boats are narrow and kind of tippy."

George and Patrick decided to take the first shift, with George at the oars. Patrick opened a can of Bullmoose and handed it to George.

"Your minimum daily requirement of barley," he explained. George began rowing and sipping, and within minutes Patrick felt a jarring strike and set the hook. Something big took off for deeper water, bending the rod and pulling line off the reel against the whine of the drag.

"Jesus, George, follow him!" Patrick yelled. "I'm running out of line!" George rowed hard in pursuit, and when they were a hundred yards from shore the fish began to tire.

Patrick started winching it up from the depths. "What is this thing?" he asked. "I can't stand the suspense." He stood up to get a better look at the fish, executing some fast footwork to keep his balance.

"Dammit, Georgie, it's a lake trout and it's four feet long. Gimme the net!"

But the trout wasn't ready to be netted. It got its second wind and began thrashing back and forth across the bow. With the rod in one hand and the net in the other, Patrick lunged at it and the boat rocked violently.

"Sit down, sit down, for Chrissake sit down!" George shouted. But Patrick was concentrating on his fish. "Come to papa, you Canadian son-of-a-bitch!" he hollered.

George looked toward the shore and saw to his horror that they had an audience; heads were poking out of the windows and doors of the cabins. Patrick leaned far to the left, got the net under the fish, and began to lift it, tipping the boat nearly on its beam-ends. George leaned right to counterbalance Patrick—and fell overboard.

Water went up his nose and roared in his ears. When he surfaced he grabbed the gunwale. "Row us in, Patrick—this water is cold!" he gasped. But Patrick was laughing too hard to row.

"This is gonna make the story of a lifetime," he said. "Here I am, minding my own business, calmly playing a fish, and all of a sudden Georgie is over the side. A lot of bubbles come up, then a beer can, then a pipe and a tobacco tin, and finally Georgie himself, blowing like a dolphin. I tell ya, it's a masterpiece!"

Patrick scooped up the can and George's pipe and tobacco with the landing net and rowed back to the ramp, towing George. When they reached the landing an aging handyman wearing a tartan tam-o'-shanter gave the trout a cursory glance.

"Just got the one, eh?" he asked. Patrick lifted the trout for all to see, but no one else came to admire it.

"Kind of standoffish, these Canadians," he said. "You don't catch a fish this big every day, even up here. You'd think some of the others would at least have a look."

"Patrick, you know how sound carries over water," George said. "When you called that fish a Canadian son-of-a-bitch they all heard you and they're probably insulted. And on a Sunday morning, too. So much for the contemplation."

"Mercy!" said Patrick. "Poor delicate Canucks. If they hang around me, they'll hear a lot worse than that."

Duncan Ross had heard and seen everything. His wife joined him at the window, and they watched as George poured water out of his shoes and squelched into the cabin.

"Well!" Ross said. "A sip of brandy after dinner is one thing, but getting drunk and falling out of a boat at eight in the morning is another. And such language! We'll have to pray very hard, my dear."

"For the Yanks?"

"No, for ourselves," said Duncan. "What with one thing and another, I suspect this week will try our souls."

After George dried off and changed clothes, he filleted the trout and warmed up canned spaghetti for lunch. When their plates were clean they poured cups of coffee.

"Did you guys hear anything moving around behind the cabin last night?" Patrick asked. "I went out to the can about midnight and I could swear I heard something big rustling around in the underbrush, and I sure as hell don't want to surprise a bear in the dark. I brought my big five-cell flashlight, but the batteries are shot. You guys go fishing tomorrow, and I'll drive out to the highway and get some fresh ones at the gas station."

That night George broiled lake trout steaks and fried some potatoes for supper. Then they drew the window blinds, opened cans of ale, lit cigars, and played stud poker for pocket change until Patrick had won it all.

"Forbidden fruit is the sweetest," he said, blowing a smoke ring and polishing off another Bullmoose. "It's kind of stimulating to sneak a drink and a cigar right under the nose of the Right Reverend Ross. Makes me feel like a schoolboy again."

"What makes me feel like a schoolboy," said Theron, "are those two girls next door. If only I were seventy again!"

By ten o'clock they were in bed. But it was a warm night, and Patrick tossed and turned. Finally he opened the drapes on his bedroom windows to admit the breeze, folded down the blankets, and covered himself with the sheet. He closed his eyes, and as he was dropping off to sleep he heard noises outside his bedroom window, just like the night before. There were whispers and then a giggle.

"Bears might whisper, but they sure as hell don't giggle," Patrick thought to himself. "I'll bet it's those girls." He opened his eyes and saw the outlines of two heads peering through the window.

Slowly and carefully, Patrick picked up his flashlight from the bedside table and pointed it at the window.

"It's those damned bears again!" he cried out in a great voice. "Is this shotgun loaded?"

There were squeals and crashes and cries of pain as the girls fled, tripping over roots and rocks. Then Patrick heard a screen door slam, followed by the irate roaring of the girls' father, Angus MacGregor. He was a stern lay preacher from Winnipeg with a beard like a prophet.

"What's going on?" he yelled. "Where were you girls?"

"It was the man from cabin seven," said one of the twins. "The tall one. He chased us. And he's got a gun!"

"I'll have his guts for a necktie," MacGregor rumbled.

The commotion awakened Duncan Ross. He came running, his bathrobe flapping. "Don't go near those men, Angus," he said. "They're from Chicago, and they may be capable of anything!" Up and down the lakeshore, cabin doors were opening and curious Canadians were converging on cabin seven.

George pulled on his trousers, went outside, and confronted Reverend Ross.

"Dammit," he said, "we've had enough foolishness for one day. Get everybody to come down to the fire ring. We have to talk."

When the company was assembled, George quieted them down and took charge.

"First of all, we haven't got a shotgun, and we don't chase teen-aged girls, even when they look in our windows.

"My cousin Patrick sells used cars, Uncle Theron is a retired professor, and I used to be a copy editor on the *Chicago Sun-Times*," George said. "Patrick talks faster than he listens, and we didn't realize this was a church camp until we saw your sign out on the highway. If you prefer, we'll leave in the morning."

But Canadians are friendly and reasonable people when politics aren't involved, and in a few minutes the situation was clarified to everyone's satisfaction. Patrick apologized for calling his trout a Canadian son-of-a-bitch. "Nothing personal," he added.

"I believe we have an apology to make, as well," said Elizabeth MacGregor. "Sarah and Emily, were you telling the truth? Did this man chase you?"

The girls looked down. "No, mother," said Sarah. "No, mother," said Emily.

Then Agatha Ross spoke up. "Duncan," she said, "it's been quite an evening. I think a nightcap may be in order." At this cue, the campers went to their cabins and returned with teacups and a surprising number of bottles. The moon was down, and glass and china clinked as drinks were poured in the faint starlight.

Angus MacGregor took a swallow from his teacup and coughed. "Elizabeth, this tastes like brandy and clam juice."

"I couldn't see the labels, Angus. But drink it down. I've got Scotch and V8!"

Patrick popped the top on a can of Bullmoose. "Not exactly expert drinkers, are they, Georgie?" he whispered. "But of course they're Scots and lack the experience of us Irish."

Monday dawned clear and cool, the first day of a week of good fishing and superlative weather. The events of the previous night were forgotten, and in a gesture of modesty and international accord, Sarah and Emily wore baggy sweatshirts and Bermuda shorts. The campfire programs led by the Americans avoided the Bible but turned out to be the high point of the week. On Monday night, George taught a class in headline writing, calling it the world's most difficult word game, and Theron's lecture on the minor Elizabethan poets drew a round of polite applause. On Tuesday, Patrick's two-hour course on how to buy a used car was a solid hit.

Wednesday was July first and Canada Day. When the campers gathered at the waterfront, a seminarian from Saskatoon brought a guitar from his cabin, and they all sang along until the liquor gave out. Then Duncan led them in a rendition of "O Canada." Patrick sang louder than anyone.

"Dammit, Pat, you're the firs' Yank I ever came across who knew the words to our national anthem," said Angus MacGregor, his words slurred by about a pint of inner peace. "Didja learn it in school?"

"No, they sing it at all the Blackhawks games, and I've got a season ticket."

"Hey, a man after my own heart! I didn't really mean it about your guts an' all. Didja ever see Bobby Hull play?"

"Sure," replied Patrick, handing Angus a Bullmoose. "The Golden Jet. And Gordie Howe, and Gump Worsley—all those guys."

"Lissen, Pat, confidenshly, do you think the '67 Maple Leafs really shoulda won the Stanley Cup, or were the Canadiens better?"

"Well, there are two schools of thought about that . . ." And all was well at Caribou Camp for the rest of the week.

George, Patrick, and Theron crossed the border into Minnesota at noon on Saturday.

"Wow, that's a relief," George said, as they pulled out of International Falls. "I've been watching the mirror for the Mounties all the way. Do you realize we were so busy fishing that we forgot to buy licenses?"

"Well, we're safely across the border now," Theron said.

"Yeah, but it's not over yet," said George. "When we went through customs I told them we didn't have anything to declare. But I forgot that there's a whole box of Cuban cigars under my seat, and it's illegal to bring them into the country. Now I'm watching for the Border Patrol. I won't feel safe until I'm back at Coot Lake."

Patrick and Theron headed home to Chicago the following Monday. After supper that night, Helen opened the refrigerator. "There's one can of that Canadian ale left," she said. "Do you want it, George?"

"Sure, let's split it." George poured the ale into two glasses and took them into the living room.

"Thanks, Helen, for putting up with all this. Did things go OK while I was gone?"

"By and large," said Helen. "But there was one disappointment— our forty-fifth anniversary was Thursday, and it was the first time we weren't together for an anniversary."

"And I'll bet you thought I forgot," George said. "The forty-fifth is the sapphire anniversary. I couldn't afford a sapphire, but I got something blue."

Behind the bar were two cardboard boxes. George handed one of them to Helen, and she removed a blue teacup wrapped in a crumpled page of the Sunday Toronto *Globe and Mail*.

"It's Wedgwood Jasperware, the same as the one I broke," said George.

"Oh, it is, it is!" Helen exclaimed. She took the cup into the dining room and compared it to five similar cups in the china cabinet. "It's a perfect match."

She returned to the living room and carefully set the cup on the bar. The Wedgwood tea service for six had been her mother's.

"I found it in an antique shop in Kenora," George said. "I'll never forget how you cried when I dropped that cup. I've been reluctant to wash dishes ever since."

Helen wrapped George in a hug. "You're forgiven, and from now on you can wash dishes without fear." She looked up at George with a coy smile. "I hate to seem greedy, George, but aren't you forgetting something? There's another box back there."

George unwrapped the second box and held it out to Helen. "Actually, this is mine, but as Patrick says, you're the best thing that ever happened to me, so you're welcome to it.

"Here you go, kiddo—have a cigar!"

Pennies from Heaven

///

*O*n a sunny afternoon in June, George was up a ladder, puttying a loose pane of glass in one of the lodge's south windows.

As he worked he pondered the mystery of mortality. Trim and strait-laced men he knew were dropping like flies in their sixties, while others who specialized in riotous living seemed to go on forever. It hardly seemed fair. His uncle Tim, for example, had died peacefully a couple of weeks previously after ninety-four happy years of hard drinking in Boston. "Makes you wonder," George thought.

He also wondered about luck, and why he never seemed to have any. "Every week for six years I buy a dollar's worth of lottery tickets at the gas station, and do I win anything? No, not a red cent. And then that dipso Heine Lipschultz buys one lousy ticket and wins seven grand! They talk about the luck of the Irish, but you couldn't prove it by me. Maybe I should change gas stations."

Helen came outside to check on him. "How's it going?" she asked.

"Bor-ring. Country life in Door County is not very exciting today."

Helen sat down on the porch steps. "Well, George, if it's excitement you're after, I can oblige you. There's something we need to talk about."

"Oh-oh," George said. "Now what?"

"It's not the end of the world, but our food budget is in trouble. Ever since you volunteered to do the grocery shopping, we've been in the red almost every month. You buy too many things that aren't on the list, and most of the time you don't compare prices or use the coupons I send along.

"Take last week, for instance. I asked you to get bread, and you brought home a crusty little fencepost that cost four dollars. I almost broke a tooth on it. I gave you coupons for Hills Brothers coffee and you got Jamaica Blue Mountain for nine dollars a pound. I asked for Kraft singles and you bought a piece of three-year-old cheddar that cost twelve dollars."

"Sure was good, though, wasn't it?" said George. "If I'm going to clog up my arteries, I might as well do it with cheese that's got some bite to it."

"Well, it bit us right in the you-know-what. We can't afford it."

"OK, I get the message," George said. "My trouble is that I've got a good sense of smell. I can scent hot french bread at a hundred yards and track it down like Lloyd's bloodhound. If I'm in the coffee aisle when somebody is grinding nice oily dark roast, I'm helpless. And I hate messing around with all those coupons at the checkout. It makes me feel like I'm on food stamps."

"Well, we will be on food stamps if you keep buying twelve-dollar cheese."

"All right," said George, "from now on I'll go grocery shopping after lunch, when I'm not hungry. How about that?"

"That might be a good start, but what about your Sunday newspaper habit? You like to drive into town on Sunday morning to buy the paper. That's fine, but do you get the Green Bay paper? No, you do not. You get the Sunday *New York Times*, all four pounds of it, and you know it takes us two weeks to read it all. We keep falling behind—it's June, and you're still doing the crosswords from April."

"I can't help myself," George said. "The *Times* smells good, too. I spent thirty-two years working for a newspaper, and when I smell ink and newsprint I rear up like an old fire horse when the alarm bell rings."

"I understand that, George, and if it were just the newspaper, I wouldn't complain. But I can't trust you in bookstores, either. The last time we went to Barnes & Noble, you spent like a drunken sailor."

George snorted derisively. "Hah! When's the last time you saw a drunken sailor buy the collected novels of Anthony Trollope?"

"All right, have it your way—you spend like a drunken reader of long-winded Victorians. The fact remains that you've got Republican tastes and a Democratic wallet, and it's killing us. Every time we have lunch at Al Johnson's you get a double order of pancakes and Swedish meatballs, and that adds up, too. But your greatest triumph was last August. You went to Sturgeon Bay for an oil change and came back with a different truck!"

"I was stimulating the economy," George said. "And I did a better job than the politicians."

"Well, just think about it, please. You aren't very good at handling money. You get carried away, and it's got to stop, unless you come up with some pennies from heaven."

George sensed that Helen's critique was winding down, so he quickly changed the subject.

"I think the mail has come. How about fetching it while I trim this putty?"

When Helen came back from the mailboxes, George was sitting on the porch steps, smoking his pipe.

"More excitement," said Helen. "A fishing catalog and a flyer from somebody who wants to sell you a hearing aid. But there's also an insured package from Boston. Who do you know in Boston?"

"Nobody, since Uncle Tim died. Let me see it."

George looked at the return address and turned to Helen with a wild surmise. "It's from Peabody and Hopgood, Attorneys-at-Law. Maybe Tim left us some money!"

George tore open the package and found three numbered envelopes. Number one was made of a heavy, creamy paper that suggested custom-tailored suits, degrees from Harvard, and paneled offices with a view of Boston Common. It demanded respectful handling, and George carefully slit it with his pocketknife.

"Well, cross your fingers," he said.

Dear Mr. O'Malley:

The firm of Peabody and Hopgood shares your
sorrow upon the passing of your uncle Timothy
M. Reilly of Boston, Massachusetts. As you
may know, he died at the Shady Villa nursing
home while watching his beloved Red Sox beat
the Yankees on television.

We are forwarding a medal that he left you
in his will, an appraisal of the medal, and
a recent letter to you that Tim was writing
when he died. Please accept our condolences
at this time of loss.

Sincerely,
Ernest Hopgood

"So much for the fortune," said George. "The medal is probably a Saint Christopher. Dad used to say Tim was a pretty free spender, and I don't expect there was much left when he died. He had season tickets to the Red Sox and divided his time between Fenway Park and a bar he owned around the corner. He just went back and forth. I don't know what he did in the winter—drink, I suppose. Well, let's see what we got."

George opened envelope number two. It contained a flat leather box and an appraisal letter. In the box was an ornate Maltese cross attached to a red, white, and black ribbon, and a second letter typed in German. George unfolded the appraisal letter.

To Whom It May Concern:

In the opinion of Rembert Hessel, Appraiser
and Broker of Militaria, the enclosed medal
is a fine example of the Knight's Cross of
the Iron Cross with oak leaves and swords,
one of the highest medals for valor awarded
by the German armed forces during World
War II.

It is in its original leather presentation case and its condition is mint. The letter indicates that the medal was presented to SS Standartenfuhrer Erwin von Diemann in 1944. Only about 7,000 Knight's Crosses in various classes were given to German soldiers and sailors during the war, and very few with oak leaves and swords. Reproductions abound, but genuine, original Knight's Crosses in this condition and with this sort of provenance rarely show up in the collector's market. I would value this one at $3,000, although it could bring more at auction.

Yours truly,
Rembert Hessel

"Kiddo," George said, "it pays to stay alive, just to see what happens next. You wanted money and I wanted luck, and now we've got a little of both, courtesy of Uncle Tim."

Envelope number three was addressed in a shaky, spidery longhand:

George T. O'Malley
Baileys Harbor
Wisconsin
PERSONAL AND CONFIDENTIAL

George took out his pocketknife again and slit the envelope.

Dear George:
If you are reading this letter, I'm dead. But as I write it, I'm still alive after a fashion. I've been in a nursing home for a month, and I've got to say, for what they charge they could stock a better grade of nurse. The ones assigned to me

are built like opera singers, and sound like them too. But they do have cable TV here, and I can watch all the Red Sox games.

Anyway, I am your uncle Tim Reilly. Your mother was my little sister. You and I never met, but you are my only living nephew, and so I have remembered you in my will.

I've given you a German medal, and it's a pretty fancy one. You'll probably want to sell it, and I wouldn't blame you if you did. The proceeds will make a nice little nest egg.

You didn't know my father, of course, but he was a lawyer in Boston and he wanted me to go to law school. But in the late thirties, everybody knew that war with Germany was coming, so I majored in German instead.

After Pearl Harbor I tried to enlist, but I was 4F because of a bad ankle. I got spiked covering second in a high school baseball game, and the ankle was always stiff after that. Eventually I wound up in an outfit called the Office of Strategic Services, which later became the CIA. Mostly, I worked as an interpreter when German officers were being interrogated, and that's how I came by the medal.

One day in March 1945, the MPs captured an SS Colonel in full dress uniform. He drove right up to our lines in a Mercedes staff car and handed over his Luger and his little SS dagger. It was obvious he wanted to surrender to us before the Russians got him, but he was one of those arrogant Prussian bastards and wouldn't admit it.

When I spoke German to him, he made fun of my accent. I said of course I had an accent, I was from Boston. He started speaking better English than I did, just to insult me, and he made some smartass remarks about Ted Williams and the Red Sox. Turned out he had relatives living on Commonwealth Avenue, and he thought he knew all about Boston and the Sox. Well, nobody can badmouth Teddy Ballgame in my presence and get away with it. I decided then and there I was going to make him pay.

His index finger had yellow nicotine stains on it, so I could tell he was a heavy smoker. I took his cigarettes away, and after three days, he was so desperate that he offered to trade me a Knight's Cross for a carton of Luckies. We weren't supposed to take decorations from prisoners of war, but I figured I was buying this one, if only for a buck fifty, which is what they were charging for a carton of cigarettes at the PX. But when I brought him the Luckies, he didn't take off the cross that was hanging around his neck. Instead he gave me a brand-new one that he had in his tunic pocket. Must have been his Sunday-go-to-meeting Knight's Cross. And there was a letter in the case from his CO—too bad it wasn't signed by Himmler, but you can't have everything. Anyway, we made the swap. Big tough SS man. He's probably dead of lung cancer by now.

After VE Day it was almost two months before I could hop a plane home. While I was waiting I played poker seven days a week, and I eventually won enough to buy a bar when I got back to Boston.

Well, that's what I did in the war, George. The only medal I ever got was from a Nazi, and I had *to pay for it. I'll close because the ball game is starting, Sox and the Yankees. I'll finish this when the game is over.*

Later—
Tim

There was a crunch of tires on gravel as Emma Olson drove up the driveway. "Are you ready, Helen?" she called out. "Shopping time!"

Helen went into the lodge and got her purse. "I'll be back in a couple of hours, George."

"OK," George replied. "Don't get carried away."

"Why not?" said Helen with a smile. "I can afford it now."

When Helen and Emma had gone, George called Harvey Dowd, an old pal of his on the *Sun-Times*.

"Hey, Harvey, do you still collect military stuff? Because if you do, I've got a Knight's Cross with oak leaves and swords, perfect and still in the box. You interested?"

"Hell, George, that would be too rich for my blood, but there's a big collectors' show in town in a couple of weeks, and you could probably sell it there. Give me a call and I'll buy you a beer."

That evening, George took a long look at the medal and told Helen about the show.

"Sell it!" she said. "I wouldn't give it house room. God only knows what that officer did to earn it."

"My sentiments exactly. Maybe I can swap it for something American."

"Like American money."

The day before the show, George and Helen drove to Evanston to visit Bill, Josie, and their grandson, Willie.

"If I can get a good price for the medal," said George, "I'll start a college fund for Willie. But I wonder how to invest the money—nothing's paying any interest these days."

The next morning, as George was leaving for the show, Helen drew him aside and spoke in low tones.

"Good luck, George—promise me you won't get carried away."

But when George returned late in the afternoon, he was carrying a box and several bags.

"George!" Helen scolded. "You promised!"

"I didn't get carried away. I was cool, calm, and collected. It took me all day, but I worked a bunch of trades, and look what I got! Three bats autographed by Ted Williams and actually used in games—you can still smell the pine tar on them—plus four autographed Spalding baseballs, an eight-by-ten glossy of Ted flipping off a sportswriter from the *Boston Globe*, and a hundred bucks left over.

"I made out like a bandit, Uncle Tim would approve, Ted Williams would approve, and baseball collectibles are appreciating a lot faster than CDs. Did someone say I couldn't handle money?"

Helen pressed her hands together in a prayerful gesture. "Thanks for the pennies from heaven, Uncle Tim," she said. "It's too bad we never got to know you."

"Well, there's one thing we know for sure," said George. "There is such a thing as the luck of the Irish after all, and Uncle Tim had it.

"Think about it—he got through the war in one piece, he was a good poker player, he had season tickets to the Red Sox, he owned a bar, he died watching the Sox beat the Yankees—and he never got married. If that's not lucky, what is?"

"George, what's the name of the medal they give to the wounded?"

"The Purple Heart."

"Any more comments like that, and you'll be eligible for one."

They got back to the lodge late the following evening. George went outside for some fresh air and a smoke while Helen unpacked their suitcases. When he went into the bedroom, he found that Helen had laid out fresh pajamas for him.

"Almost forty-six years together and I still get treated like royalty," George thought. "I've got no business complaining about my luck."

He looked at his bedside table and saw a red ribbon tied in a bow and held together with a safety pin.

"What's this, Helen?"

"It's a good conduct medal. I award it to husbands I like."

"What do I do to earn it?"

"Oh, I'll think of something," Helen said.

The Four Musketeers

///

A steady rain was drumming on the roof of Coot Lake Lodge.
George put his empty coffee cup in the sink, lit his pipe, and went
out onto the porch to look for a patch of blue in the west. But the
late August sky was uniformly gray, and there would be no fishing
today.

Helen had been doing the laundry in the basement. "Is it still
raining?" she asked when she came back upstairs.

"Like a cow pissing on a flat rock!"

"George, promise me you won't say things like that at our
class reunion. It's our fiftieth, and we're going. I just filled out the
reservation form."

"OK, I'll be genteel," George said. He went back into the kitchen
and looked at the list of chores Helen had compiled after breakfast
that morning. Most of them involved varnish.

"It's too humid to varnish today," he told her. "It'll never dry. I'll
fix my turntable instead."

George had a large collection of LP records dating back to the
fifties, and listening to them was one of his major pleasures. But
the turntable that had once spun his records at a steady $33^1/3$
revolutions per minute had become erratic. Sometimes it ran
fast and made the Four Freshmen sound like Alvin and the Chip-
munks. When it ran slow, Count Basie's band seemed to be playing
underwater.

It had taken George the better part of a day in Green Bay to find
a new motor and drive belt, so to be on the safe side he had bought
two of each. He disconnected the turntable and carried it to the bar

by the windows overlooking the lake, where Helen was writing checks and stuffing them into envelopes.

"Oh, good," she said. "Now I'll be able to play my Kingston Trio records again. The last time I tried they sounded like grand opera."

"Which was probably an improvement." He and Helen had roughly similar tastes, but they disagreed on folk music. Helen remembered it fondly from her college days in the sixties. George remembered it too, but not fondly. He suspected that most folk music had been written by folks from the East Village who had never been west of Central Park.

Replacing the motor and belt turned out to be a simple job, requiring only a big screwdriver and a little bad language. George hooked up the turntable and found a Kingston Trio record.

"OK, Helen, if you insist, I'll play some of this, but not 'Scotch and Soda.' You know how that one goes: 'Scotch and soda, jigger of gin . . .' Anybody who would mix scotch and gin would drink his own bathwater."

George let the Trio plunk through a couple of tunes, and then he pulled a Frank Sinatra record out of the cabinet. "Old Blue Eyes will be the real test," he said, and gently dropped the needle on the first track. But he was playing the wrong side of the record.

> Laura is the face in the misty light,
> Footsteps that you hear down the hall,
> The laugh that floats on a summer night,
> That you can never quite recall.
>
> And you see Laura on a train that is passing through,
> Those eyes, how familiar they seem,
> She gave your very first kiss to you—
> That was Laura, but she's only a dream.

George lifted the needle and stood looking out the window. "Laura" always reminded him of high school and Laura Lemerond the cheerleader, his steady girl when she was seventeen and blonde and bouncy, with big blue eyes and a high-pitched laugh.

"I wonder what ever happened to her?" George thought. "She just kind of disappeared in '61 or '62. My God, it's been a long time—I suppose she's gray and worn out like the rest of us."

George shrugged and put Dave Brubeck's *Jazz Goes to College* on the turntable. Brubeck always cheered him up.

After supper that night George fixed the dripping faucet in the upstairs bathroom. While he was working, Helen played a Billie Holiday record.

> My old flame,
> I can't even think of his name,
> But it's funny now and then,
> How my thoughts go flashing back again,
> To my old flame . . .

When Billie had wrung every drop of longing from the song, Helen put the record back in its jacket, unaware that George had been listening from the top of the stairs.

"Coming to bed, George?"

"OK, in a little bit."

He stood by the west windows and looked across the lake. The sky was beginning to clear, and the moon was racing through ragged clouds.

"Her old flame, eh?" George thought. "Richie. Richie Richards, the football hero. Richie, the most likely to succeed. Probably making millions and handsome as ever." Richie was the last person George wanted Helen to be reunited with.

Upstairs, Helen was brushing her hair and thinking about Laura.

"I wonder what she looks like now. Glamorous, I suppose, for her age. She had small bones, and women like her tend to keep their looks if they don't put on too much weight."

Helen wondered about Richie, too. "His hair was thinning even in high school, and big men like him go to seed pretty fast. I might not even recognize him."

As the weeks before the Sturgeon Bay Class of 1960 reunion went by, George almost succeeded at putting Laura and Richie out of his mind. But then, one Saturday morning, Helen came down the stairs from the attic.

"George, guess what! I found our high school yearbooks." She put them on the bar by the window while George brought in the coffeepot. Helen began to read her yearbook page by page, but George flipped through his at a faster pace, passing over the stilted articles and staged photographs until he found the blank pages where his classmates had written personal messages.

Richie's message to him was written with red ink in a round, childish hand. "Hey Georgie," it read, "too bad you didnt make the football team, but your the best sports writer we ever had. CU a round, Yrs truly, Richie."

"That's him all over," George thought. "Couldn't spell his way through a book of cigarette papers, but he had to rub it in about the football team. Could I help it if I was too skinny?"

George found the message he had really been looking for on the last page. The writing was small and intensely feminine, with little hearts instead of dots over the *i*'s.

"Georgie," it said, "I don't know what to write, but you know what I'm thinking. You're the one who's good with words! And other things. Love, Laura XXXX."

George's heart beat a little faster as he read the message a second time, and he abandoned all hope of forgetting about Laura and Richie. When Helen went shopping in Baileys Harbor that afternoon, George found her yearbook and read two of the messages.

"Helen," Richie's message read, "so glad U are going to Madison this fall. So am I, and we can pick up where we left off. U know what I mean. Isle view, Richie."

George had been a copy editor for thirty-two years, and "Isle view" offended him. "What a jerk," he thought, "and a trite jerk to boot. If he gets out of line at the reunion, I'll tell him where to go."

Laura's message to Helen was written in a straightforward longhand without the little hearts.

"Congrats on getting into the National Honor Society," she wrote. "Looks like you, me, Georgie, and Richie are going to college together this fall. The four musketeers. But stay away from Georgie—he's my musketeer. Sincerely, Laura." With a twinge of guilt, George closed Helen's yearbook and put it back where he had found it.

Helen and George spent a lot of time on their appearance during the week before the reunion. Helen devoted a day to shopping for dresses at the tourist boutiques up and down the peninsula, and spent almost four hours at LaVerne's Salon de Beauty in Egg Harbor. When she got home from the salon, George was glad to see that her hair was still long. But its color had changed, from the familiar corn silk and gray to a shining platinum. Oddly enough, the long silver hair made Helen seem younger. Apparently LaVerne knew her business.

George didn't spend much time on his hair, what there was of it, but he rummaged through his closet and assembled a tasteful ensemble—gray flannel trousers, a button-down tattersall shirt he hadn't worn in years, a narrow tie with vaguely regimental stripes, and a deep navy blue blazer. "Classy, but not overdone," he thought. "Just like me."

On Thursday night, Helen and George went over their schedule for the weekend.

"I promised to help decorate the tables at the country club," said Helen, "so we have to be there by five tomorrow afternoon. Then there are cocktails at six, a buffet supper, and dancing."

George snorted. "I can imagine us eating and dancing, but it's hard to picture the Class of '60 drinking cocktails," he said. "We used to pound down quarts of Blatz like there was no tomorrow. In those days we wouldn't have known a cocktail from antifreeze."

"But there will be a tomorrow, so don't drink too much," Helen said, with a slight warning note in her voice. "Anyway, Saturday morning is golf, Saturday night is the Grand Ball, and Sunday is a picnic at Weborg Point."

As they walked to the door of the country club the following afternoon, George got a good look at one of Helen's new outfits from behind. It was a classic "little black dress," in a size he didn't think she could get into.

In the foyer, a classmate named Debbie Dombrowski was sitting at the registration table. She stood up, complimented Helen on her dress, and then stared appraisingly at George.

"Don't be shy, Georgie," she said. "I'm divorced but reasonably safe." She enveloped him in a hug, and when she released him she playfully straightened his tie. "Where have you been for the last fifty years?" she whispered, and winked at Helen.

George had forgotten what it was like to be flirted with, even by a woman of sixty-seven, and he found it mildly exciting. Of course, Debbie had always thrown herself at everything with pants on, but it was a good way to start the evening just the same.

"The printer was supposed to be here already with the name tags," said Debbie, "but he hasn't shown up yet. There's a couple in the bar, but I don't know who they are. Why don't you go in and talk to them, Georgie, while Helen and I start on the tables."

It was cool and dark in the bar. A man and woman were seated at the far end of the room. The man was bald and paunchy, and the woman reminded George of an aging Barbie doll, with a tight sweater and a helmet of fluffy blonde hair glistening with spray.

"Hold the fort, honey," the man said. "I'm going to the john." He walked rapidly toward the door, but as he passed George he stopped short.

"Georgie? Georgie O'Malley? Chrissake, don't you recognize me? It's Richie!"

George stared at him. Sure enough, under the flabby cheeks and wispy mustache was a ghost of the old, handsome Richie. They shook hands and smiled uncertainly at each other.

"Hey, Georgie, do me a favor and keep Laura company for a minute, will ya? You two probably have a lot to talk over."

George turned and looked at the woman sitting at the bar. "Laura?" he asked. "You mean Laura Lemerond? I haven't seen her since our freshman year of college. She's your wife?"

"Yeah," said Richie. "Didn't you know? In '61, I blew out a knee in the April scrimmages and lost my football scholarship. Then I got drafted and Laura and I got married—it was all kind of sudden. I put in my twenty years in the army and now I'm working in a sporting goods store in Milwaukee. Lemme know if you need a boat or a shotgun or anything." Richie pulled a Marlboro from a pack in his shirt pocket and headed for the door.

Laura was staring into a Tom Collins. George sat down next to her. She glanced at him, and then her eyes widened and a smile wrinkled her makeup.

"Georgie, my old flame Georgie." She put her hand on George's wrist and then slowly withdrew it.

"Remember this, Georgie?" She hopped off her bar stool and did a dancer's pirouette that lifted the hem of her pleated skirt above the knee. "Not bad for an old lady, am I? It's my cheerleading outfit. I had to let out the skirt a little, but the sweater still fits."

"Yeah, it sure does," said George. He hadn't imagined meeting Laura this way, in a dark, deserted bar, with her smelling faintly of gin and spinning around in an overstuffed Sturgeon Bay Clippers cheerleading sweater. George remembered how proud she had been when the sweaters were handed out and she was the only girl on the cheerleading squad who needed an extra-large.

Laura took a sip of her drink and looked up at George, inviting a kiss. But before anything could happen, Helen came into the bar. Richie was right behind her. He took a long look and froze.

"My God," he said. "Is that you, Helen?" Helen turned and Richie looked her up and down, whistled, and walked toward her, his arms outstretched.

"Careful, Richie," George warned.

Laura looked at George and laughed her old soprano laugh. "Georgie O'Malley," she said, "you're jealous. You're jealous of Richie after fifty years. Helen, you are a lucky woman."

The four of them talked during the cocktail hour and sat together at dinner. For the ball Saturday night, Helen wore another new dress, made of some kind of clinging, glittering deep green material that swished as she walked and made it obvious that a slender and well-proportioned woman was inside. It was accented with a loose silver belt that hung low on her hips and matched the color of her hair. Obviously, Helen knew her business too.

George danced with Laura, and Richie danced with Helen. For the rest of the weekend Laura and Richie stuck to Helen and George like flypaper. "We're still the four musketeers," Laura said, and laughed that laugh again.

After the picnic on Sunday, the musketeers parted with handshakes and hugs.

When George and Helen got back to the lodge, George built a fire in the fireplace, loosened his tie, and flopped down on one of the old couches. Helen joined him. Nothing was said for a few minutes, but they both knew the reunion wasn't quite over yet.

"So tell me, Helen, what did you think of Laura?" George asked.

"You want the truth?"

"Sure."

"She still wants to be the high school queen, and she still wants everybody to stare at her. She was wearing so much wire under that old sweater of hers, she'd set off the alarm in an airport. And that screechy laugh was about to drive me crazy. Now I suppose I've hurt your feelings."

"Not much," George said. "She screeched like that when she was seventeen, but I thought it was cute. And I never got to find out what she was wearing under her sweater, then or now."

Helen smiled at George. "Glad to hear it. Does you credit."

"And as for Richie," said George, "he's a perfect match for her. He's a decent guy, but all he can talk about is his old football games. They're both living in 1960, and they're welcome to it. Thank God you and I are growing old gracefully."

"Well, I'm not as graceful as I used to be," Helen said. "All that jitterbugging was getting me in the small of the back. And if I hear 'Rock Around the Clock' one more time I'll be sick."

"Me, too. But listen, Helen, I've got to know—did Richie try anything while I wasn't looking?"

"Not once," replied Helen. "I was a little disappointed. Did Laura?"

"She puckered up when we first met in the bar, but nothing came of it."

Helen sighed. "Let's face it, George, our old flames have gone out."

"And it's a great relief," George said. "Looks like we're stuck with each other for a while."

Helen took George's hand and the two of them stared into the fire. Then she broke the silence.

"Come on, George—you were still attracted to Laura, weren't you?"

"To the memory of her, sure," George said. "But a weekend with the real thing cured me—that and watching you walk around in your new dresses. Be honest, Helen. You bought them for Richie to look at, didn't you?"

"Don't be silly," said Helen. "Women don't wear dresses like that for men; they wear them for other women. I bought those outfits just in case I had to show Laura she had some competition. Ridiculous, wasn't I? But I'll wear them again, just for you, if you'll promise me something."

"Name it."

"When the credit card bill comes, let me open it. Those dresses were expensive."

George grinned at her. "Tell you what, Helen, I'll overlook the dresses if you'll overlook an outboard motor. Just a small one. Richie can get it for me wholesale."

"Oh, I suppose," Helen said.

As they went up the stairs, Helen had a final question.

"George, we barely knew each other in high school, and there's something else I've been meaning to ask you. Did you ever try out for the football team?"

"Yeah, but I didn't make the cut," said George. "I was too skinny. Did you ever try out for cheerleading?"

Helen laughed. "I wanted to, but my dad wouldn't allow it. He said the skirts were too short. But it was probably just as well that I didn't. I was skinny, too. Still am."

George put his arm around Helen's waist.

"I'll be the judge of that," he said.

Let George Do It

The three-day windstorm that struck Wisconsin in late October 2010 left thousands of people without power for days. It uprooted trees and wrenched the roofs from buildings. Southwest winds that reached sixty miles an hour sent huge waves rolling up Green Bay and crashing into the Door County shoreline. Boats and docks were damaged, and residents of the county talked about the storm for weeks.

"It's a sign of global warming," said the liberals.

"We never had weather like this when Bush was president," said the conservatives.

On the second night of the storm, when the winds were at their height, George O'Malley couldn't sleep. The lodge's old timbers were creaking like the ribs and rigging of a wooden sailing ship in heavy weather, and the building seemed to shiver on its foundations when the heaviest gusts went roaring through. He got out of bed without waking Helen, put on jeans and a wool shirt, and went downstairs. Russell jumped off the end of the bed, yawned, stretched, and followed him.

In the kitchen, George poured the last of that morning's pot of coffee into a mug and heated it in the microwave. "At least we still have electricity," he thought, "for the time being, anyway."

George lit his pipe, picked up a copy of the *Door County Journal* that Helen had left on the kitchen table, and took the coffee into the living room. The chimney flue was growling and grumbling, the south-facing windows were rattling, and the wind whined and whimpered around the eaves and overhangs.

"Sounds like the banshees have come to get me," he muttered, and sat down on a sofa in front of the fireplace. He looked at the *Journal* and made a sour face. The entire front page above the fold was devoted to a picture of Gordon Sligh, a handsome, jut-jawed merchant and real estate broker who had won a Man of the Year award from the local Commerce Club. Under the picture was a long story about his great success, charitable works, religious zeal, and right-wing politics.

"Easy for him to be charitable," George thought. "He owns half of the county. Just once, I'd like to see an ordinary joe win an award—a small businessman like Bump, maybe."

George flipped to the sports section and immersed himself in a story about the Packers. He was startled when Helen touched his shoulder.

"Are you all right, sweetheart?" she asked. Dressed in slippers, pajamas, and a bathrobe, she had padded silently down the stairs to see where he was.

"Yeah, I'm fine," George replied. "But it sounds like the house is about to blow away." He took a sip of coffee and stuck out his tongue. "And this stuff tastes like transmission fluid. I'll put on the kettle for some tea," he said.

Metallic clanks and crashes from outside interrupted him. "Now what? That sounded expensive—I'd better go and look."

George put on a down vest and a ball cap, turned on the outside lights, and called Russell. "C'mon, old puppy," he said. "Let's see what's going on."

Out on the porch the wind was cold and wet and almost pushed George off his feet. He soon saw what had made the noise—a gust had blown his aluminum canoe off its sawhorses and had rolled it over and over until it collided with the front bumper of his pickup truck.

George turned the canoe right side up and dragged it out of the way. Then he lifted a fifty-pound plastic bag of sunflower seed from the bed of the truck and dropped it into the canoe. "That oughta hold you," he said, puffing.

Back indoors, George poured a cup of tea and sat down on the sofa again. "No harm done, as far as I can see," he said. "The wires are all humming like mandolin strings, but they're still up. Oh, and by the way, don't pet Russell until he dries off a little. He tried to pee on his favorite box elder but he was pointing right into the wind. I don't think any of it hit the tree."

Helen went to the bookshelf and returned with a copy of James Thurber's *Fables for Our Time*. "Tell you what, George, we aren't going to get back to sleep tonight, and we haven't opened this book in years. Let's read it to each other."

But they did fall asleep, all three of them, after Helen finished the fable called "The Unicorn in the Garden," and they didn't wake up until the phone rang about seven thirty. Stiff and groggy, George rose from the couch and shuffled into the kitchen to answer it.

"Hey, George, this is Jack. I've just been outside to look at the storm damage, and I've got a problem."

Jack Paisley was a retired ore boat engineer who lived alone in a cottage on the Green Bay side of the peninsula. He was a few years older than George, but when they were boys they had spent countless hours on the school bus together. As the years passed and Jack became arthritic and a little vague, George spent more and more time helping him with yard work and household chores. The monthly meetings of the Baileys Harbor Bird and Booyah Club were among his few social contacts.

"What's the trouble, Jack?"

"You wouldn't believe it, George. You know the creek that runs through my yard and down to the bay? Well, sometime last night the wind blew a great big elm stump right into the mouth of the creek, and on top of that, the waves washed in a regular mountain of mussel shells. It's still blowing a mile a minute, and now the creek is blocked and it's flooding. My back is acting up again, and there ain't much I can do about it. I figure I've got maybe two hours before the water starts running into my basement windows, and the sump pump won't work because my power is out."

"Oh, brother," George said.

"But that's not all," said Paisley. "My latest granddaughter is getting baptized in Sturgeon Bay at nine this morning, and I absolutely have to be there. I'll probably be gone by the time you get to my place."

"Well, I'll round up Bump and we'll come over as quick as we can," offered George. "Do you think we could dig a channel with shovels and let the water out?"

"Jeez, I dunno, George. Shovels would probably take too long. You'd be better off with a trenching machine."

"I haven't got a trenching machine, but I've got Bump," George said. "He'll have to do." George called Bump, kissed Helen good-bye, and was putting on a jacket when the phone rang again.

"Hey, George, this is Hans. Have you got any room in your freezer? The wire from the transformer to our house just went down, and I'd hate to lose all my beef and frozen fish. Could you come over and get it?"

"OK, Hans, I'll be there in a minute," George said.

"Thanks, George. And one other thing—what do you do around here when the power is out? I've got no TV or Internet."

"For God's sake, Hans, read a book. Or chase Beth around. Use your imagination!"

About an hour later, George and Bump drove down the narrow driveway to Jack's cottage. Sure enough, the yard was flooded and the water had crept close to the basement windows. And Jack hadn't exaggerated—a drift of mussel shells four feet high and twenty feet long was damming the creek.

Bump shouted so George could hear him over the roar of the wind. "There's no point in messing around with shovels—we'll have to blast. My brother does the blasting at the limestone quarry, and he showed me how to do it. He's up north bow hunting this week, but he left me his keys, so lemme take your truck and I'll drive over to the quarry quick and pick up some dynamite and stuff. There's a portable generator at the quarry too—I'll bring it with me, and if nothing else we can use it to run Jack's sump pump."

Bump was back in a half hour. He and George dragged the generator across the yard, opened a basement window, and connected the generator to the sump pump with an extension cord.

"Why don't you get it started, George, just in case, and I'll wire up the dynamite. I brought a dozen sticks, and I figure that should be enough to blow up the stump and move about a ton of those mussel shells."

"You're the doctor," George said. He pulled out the choke, yanked the starter rope, and felt proud when the generator fired up on the first pull. He flipped the switch and the sump pump shot a stream of water out onto the lawn. "So far, so good," he thought.

When Bump had buried the dynamite under the stump and the mussel shells, he started walking backward with the spool of wire that connected the blasting caps to the detonator. He and George hid behind the pickup.

"Well, here goes," said Bump. "Fire in the hole!"

The first thing George felt was the vibration of the earth under his shoes, followed by a shock wave that rattled his breastbone. He peered cautiously over the bed of his truck and saw a towering fountain of smoke and water and mussel shells, still rising. He looked higher and saw something more ominous: a chunk of elm stump six feet long and a foot in diameter was spinning lazily overhead at a height of about a hundred feet. As he watched, it reached its apex and then, pushed to the north by the wind, began to fall directly toward them.

"Chrissake, Bump, run!" George shouted, but before they could move very far, the chunk of elm fell into the bed of the truck, bounced, and fell into the bed again.

"Wow!" Bump exclaimed. "That dynamite is powerful stuff. I guess I didn't need it all. But look—the shells are gone and so is the water."

"Wonderful," George said. "Now check out my truck!"

"Oh-oh," said Bump. "Gosh, you wouldn't think a couple hundred pounds of dead wood could do that much damage." The truck was sagging sadly to the rear, and the back bumper was almost touching the ground. The bed was severely dented and the rear tires were flat. George looked underneath and saw that both rear springs were broken. And then it started to rain.

Back at the lodge, Helen was taking a pan of biscuits out of the oven when the phone rang.

"You gotta aigs, Helen?" the caller asked.

It was Rosa Zamboni, a widow in her seventies and one of Door County's few Italian immigrants. She lived a stone's throw from Jack Paisley, and there was talk that they were sweet on each other. Rosa had never learned to drive, and when she needed to shop or go to the doctor, she depended on Jack to take her. When Jack's back was acting up, George drove her in Helen's old Buick wagon.

"You mean eggs? Like from a chicken?"

"*Sì*, aigs," Rosa said. "I make-a angel food cake for Jack. Twelve-a aigs. I beat, I beat, I beat. Cake, it rise pretty good, but all over sudden is sonic bomb!"

"Sonic what?"

"Sonic bomb. Big-a noise! I look in oven and cake is fall down, flat like omelet. So I gotta start over, but the market is closed. Helen, you gotta aigs?"

Helen looked in the refrigerator. "I've got eleven," she said.

"That's OK," replied Rosa. "Jack, he's-a never going to know."

"Your secret is safe with me," Helen said. "As soon as George gets back, I'll have him bring them over."

George and Bump were sitting in Jack Paisley's kitchen when Jack returned from the baptism. He thanked them profusely. "You're welcome, Jack," said George, "but now you've got to give us a ride home. My truck isn't going anywhere for a while."

When Jack dropped George off at the lodge, Helen met him at the door.

"Where's your truck?" she asked, and George told her what had happened. Helen burst out laughing.

"It's not funny," George said. "I need that truck and now I'll have to shell out a five-hundred-dollar deductible to get it fixed."

"I'm not laughing at you, George. I just realized that Bump's dynamite was Rosa Zamboni's sonic bomb. But don't sit down—you've got to take this carton of eggs over to her place. You'll have to drive the Buick."

When George returned, he flopped down on a sofa in front of the fireplace.

"What a morning! I've gone a hundred miles already. You know, Helen, I hate to say this, but sometimes I think I'm kind of taken for granted around here—just the neighborhood step-and-fetch-it. I'm always running around helping people with this and that. I don't mind, but does anybody ever stop to think that I might be busy sometimes?"

November went by and half of December, and the windstorm was largely forgotten. But then, a week before Christmas, George found a letter waiting for him when he returned to the lodge after a day of ice fishing on Kangaroo Lake.

The letter was from something called the Door County Civic Club. George was well up on local affairs, but he had never heard of the Door County Civic Club.

"Dear Mr. O'Malley," the letter said. "We are pleased to inform you that you have been chosen as the DCCC's Man of the Year for 2010, in recognition of your tireless and cheerful service to the community. Your friends and neighbors nominated you for this award. Enclosed please find a check for $500."

"Well, I be go to hell," said George. Before he could think of anything else to say, the doorbell rang. Rosa Zamboni came in, followed by Jack Paisley carrying a box. Rosa opened the box and took out an angel food cake, a foot high and frosted with Santas and Christmas trees.

"*Buon Natale*, Giorgio," she said. "Merry Christmas. I bring-a back the aigs."

Bump and Emma arrived next with a cast-iron skillet of walleye filets, Lloyd brought deep-fried okra, and Hans and Beth lugged a kettle of chili to the kitchen. Leroy brought a large venison roast in a Dutch oven, bubbling in red wine and onions. "You guys can't complain about this venison," he said. "It's only a week old, and the road salt preserved it real good."

"Could you give me a hand, George?" Jack asked. "I've got half a case of cherry wine cooling in the car, to drink to your health, but my back is acting up again and I don't think I can carry it."

They had supper and drank many toasts. The party broke up at about midnight, and when everyone had left George took Helen in his arms.

"You and your phony civic club," he said. "For a minute there, you had me fooled. But I'd rather get an award from the Baileys Harbor Bird and Booyah Club any day. Thanks, sweetheart. A little recognition goes a long way. I guess I'm ready for another year of stepping and fetching."

George kissed her, and was still kissing her when Hans came in from the porch.

"Oops! Sorry to interrupt, but my car won't start. George, have you got some jumper cables?"

"In a minute, Hans," said Helen. "He's busy."

Reefer Madness

Gather ye rosebuds while ye may," wrote the poet Robert Herrick, a long time ago. "That age is best which is the first, when youth and blood are warmer . . ."

Sooner or later, every man in his late sixties looks back at his warm-blooded days and wonders if he spent too many of them at work and too few at play. And he asks himself: Do I have enough bad habits?

George O'Malley is one of those men. In a modest way, his life has been a success, but achieving that success cost him a lot of fun and adventure over the years. In the 1960s, for instance, when his contemporaries were driving Volkswagen buses with daisies painted on them and killing off their brain cells with recreational chemicals, George was too broke and too square and too busy to join in.

The 1970s and '80s passed in a blur of nights on the copy desk, and in the '90s he was still working. And now that he is footloose and able to kick up his heels, he can't shake off his habitual restraint. Guinness Extra Stout is the strongest intoxicant in regular use at Coot Lake Lodge, at the rate of a bottle a day, and the only chemical on the menu is the lye in Helen's lutefisk.

But George has one redeeming fault: he smokes a pipe.

In fact, he owns about twenty pipes. He smokes them, he says, because the rituals of filling, lighting, tamping, and puffing give him time to think, and the older he gets, the more thinking he needs to do. He invests some time in contemplation almost every evening, sitting by the fireplace with a briar and a glass and a book.

Sometimes he remembers Herrick's poem and wonders if there are any rosebuds left with his name on them.

George and Helen were drying the dishes after lunch on a brilliant Saturday afternoon in May when the mailman tooted his horn and turned around in their driveway.

"I'll go fetch the mail, Helen," George said, and dropped his towel on the counter. He was back in a couple of minutes, carrying a cardboard box in one hand and a stack of junk mail in the other. He put it all on the bar by the west windows and began to sort it.

"Occupant, resident, resident, occupant. Helen, have I told you about my latest scheme to assure wealth and security in our old age?"

Helen came in from the kitchen. "No, but I have a feeling you're going to," she said.

"Actually, I thought it up just this minute," George explained. "Half of the mail we get is addressed to 'occupant' or 'resident,' right? And we just recycle most of it, so we don't make a penny on the transaction.

"Well, here's my plan—we tell the post office that I am Mr. Occupant and you are Mrs. Resident, and as soon as their computer gets the hang of it, they'll deliver all the mail addressed to 'occupant' or 'resident' in our zip code to us, bales of it, free of charge. Then we'll load it in the pickup every week, haul it to the recycler ourselves, and sell it. Even at three cents a pound, we'll be rich beyond the dreams of avarice."

Helen was a Norwegian farm girl from Peninsula Center, where money had always been in short supply. She performed a couple of quick mental calculations, rejected George's idea as unworkable, and gave him one of the indulgent smiles she had perfected when she taught second grade.

"It will never pay," she said, "and if you are Mr. Occupant and I am Mrs. Resident, what will happen to the mail addressed to O'Malley?"

George sighed. "It's a joke, Helen," he said.

Humor had been almost as scarce as money around Peninsula

Center, and Helen was still mildly suspicious of it. "Oh. Very funny," she said. "Anyway, I suppose the box is your pipe tobacco."

"Yup," George responded. "I was almost out." He opened the box with his pocketknife and took out sixteen vacuum-sealed tins of Murphy's Irish Flake, fresh from Dublin. Each tin held an ounce and three-quarters of sweet Virginia tobacco that had been pressed into a block and then cut into thin strips.

George smoked two tins of Irish Flake a week, generating 104 empty tins a year. Because neither he nor Helen ever discarded anything remotely useful, the tins accumulated and, in obedience to the second law of thermodynamics, found their way out of the lodge and around the neighborhood.

Lloyd Barnes had two or three of them, which he used to carry the hand-rolled Bugler cigarettes he smoked. Bump had several dozen filled with stray nuts and bolts. Beth used them for buttons, pins, and needles; Emma stored homegrown herbs and spices in hers; and Helen used them for postage stamps. More than once, George had opened a tin, anticipating a satisfying smoke, only to find curled-up, twenty-year-old three-cent stamps that Helen had vowed to use on a letter someday.

"What's on the docket for this afternoon, George?" Helen asked.

"I thought I'd take Russell and drive around to the north end of the swamp and see if the late warblers are coming through. I haven't seen a Connecticut or a Mourning yet, and they're overdue. I can check out our line fence while I'm at it."

George picked up a pipe and a box of matches and a tamper and a fresh tin of Irish Flake from the bar and put them in the pockets of an oversized chamois cloth shirt he wore like a jacket. He hung his binoculars around his neck and headed for the door. "I'm off to 'haunts of coot and hern,'" he recited. "Alfred, Lord Tennyson."

"What a morning!" said Helen. "First humor and then poetry. But tell me, George, I've always wondered—what's a hern?"

"A heron, I guess."

"Then why didn't he just write 'heron' and be done with it?"

"Because it had to rhyme with 'fern.' He's a poet, Helen, and an English one at that. You just have to cut him some slack."

To drive to the north side of his twenty acres, George had to take the long way around—east on Coot Lake Road to the highway, north for a mile, west on Short Cut, and then a half mile south on Town Line to a rutted tractor road that ran to the east on his side of the fence. As his pickup bounced along, he could see fresh tire tracks in the slippery clay of the tractor road.

"Russell, my boy," he said, "we've had company. Somebody else has been on this road, and not long ago. I wonder what they've been up to."

Observing a precaution of long standing, he turned around when he reached the end of the tractor road. He always turned around before leaving the truck in difficult or swampy terrain, so that if he got stuck, he would at least be headed in the right direction. No one was there, but when George trained his binoculars on the cedars in search of warblers, he noticed the glint of the afternoon sun on metal. He walked into the swamp for a closer look and found a quarter-barrel of Budweiser sitting in a steel tub of ice that had barely begun to melt.

"Well, well, Russell," he said, "here's a windfall! It makes me thirsty just to look at it." George shifted into four-wheel drive, backed his truck as close as he could, and loaded the tub, the barrel, and most of the ice into the bed.

"Finders keepers. This ought to teach people to keep off my land, don't you think? I'll invite the Bird and Booyah Club to drink it up, and you can come too, old puppy. It'll be like the beer party I never had when I was in college." Russell grinned and thumped his tail on the passenger seat. George was in a good mood, and therefore, so was he.

George's first stop was at Deputy Doug's house near the Coot Lake Road intersection. Doug was off duty that night and would be overjoyed to attend, he said. And so were Lloyd, Hans, Leroy, Jack, and Bump.

"Hey, George, do you mind if I bring my brother-in-law Byron along?" Bump asked. "He and my sister Shelley are visiting for the weekend."

"No trouble at all," George replied. "Byron and Shelley, eh? Do they have any Keats?"

"What?"

"It's a joke. But by all means bring Byron. There's a lot of beer in that keg and we'll never finish it, but he can help even up the odds a little."

Back at the lodge, George told Helen about his plans for the evening.

"Ordinarily I wouldn't approve," she said, "but everyone will be walking except Jack and Leroy, and I can be the designated driver for them. I'll make you a pizza—Rosa Zamboni gave me her recipe. There isn't time to go to the store, but I think I have most of the ingredients."

Huffing and puffing, George dragged the tub and the barrel to the shore of Coot Lake, set up eight lawn chairs, and built a campfire. Helen came down to the fire ring and handed George a bag of pretzels and a roll of paper towels.

"Helen, we won't need towels," George said.

"Oh, yes, you will, if you're going to drink beer and eat pizza and generally behave like the beasts of the field. I haven't forgotten that time last summer when your hot dog leaked mustard and you wiped your hands on Russell."

The booyah boys arrived one by one, and by sunset they were all seated around the fire. George called the meeting to order.

"We don't have any marshmallows," he said, "but we could sing 'Kumbayah.'"

There was a chorus of boos. "OK, so much for the entertainment. Let's get with it—I've got to take the barrel back to the store tomorrow, and it will be a lot easier to lift if it's empty."

"Thanks for throwing the party, George," said Lloyd. He filled a huge ceramic tankard stamped "You ain't nothin' but a hound dog—Souvenir of Graceland" and took a sip. "Who bought the beer?"

"I'm guessing it's Pinky Schroeder's beer," Deputy Doug said. "He's a good kid, by and large, but he just turned twenty-one, and most of his buddies are underage. His old man farms the plow land just north of George's, and Pinky must have been planning a little birthday party tonight, back out of sight of Town Line Road in George's swamp. So the way I figure it, Pinky was trespassing, the barrel is contraband, possession is nine-tenths of the law, and besides, we're helping him stay out of trouble. Drink it with a clear conscience."

When Helen brought them the pizza she had made, she apologized. "It probably isn't as spicy as you are used to," she said. "It's kind of a Norwegian pizza. I made it on my lefse griddle, and I didn't have any pepperoni, so I used codfish. I hope there's enough to go around."

"Well, I coulda brought some venison sausage, but I didn't because you guys are such picky eaters," Leroy said. "The last time I brought venison you all turned up your noses just because it had been lying out on 57 for a coupla days in August."

By midnight the moon was down, the world's problems had been talked over and solved, the last fragments of cold codfish pizza had been consumed, Russell, Grits, and Ollie had tired of fetching things, the ice in the tub had melted, and the beer keg was floating. The meeting was adjourned by unanimous consent, and the men stumbled up the hill to the road.

George and Russell sat alone by the dying embers of the fire. George had eaten two large slices of pizza and polished off nine plastic cups of beer. His stomach was uneasy, and the world seemed to be moving rapidly to the left. He drew another cup of beer, reached for his pipe, and noticed an Irish Flake tin on the ground a few feet away, barely visible in the firelight. He opened the tin and found that it was full of small green leaves. The fresh tin of tobacco he had opened that morning was still in his shirt pocket.

"Well, whadya know, Russell, one of my pals is a secret pothead, but what the hey, after all these years, I'll finally get to try some of it." He rubbed out half a slice of tobacco on his palm, blended in an equal amount of the green leaves, and packed the mixture into his pipe. He smoked the bowl to a fine gray ash and stared into the fire. The world was now moving to the right. George filled his pipe again.

When Helen returned after driving Jack and Leroy home, she walked down the hill from the lodge. "Have a nice party, George?" she asked, and sat down beside him.

"You bet. Bes' kinda party—totally free of charge."

He burst into song. "Totally, totally, totally, totally, life is but a dream!

"Hey, that reminds me of a joke. Thish guy gets lost in Greenwich Village an' he sees a beatnik sitting on the curb playing a guitar. So he says, Does the downtown subway run all night? An' the beatnik says, 'Doo-dah, doo-dah.' Get it? Issa musical joke."

Helen gave George a searching look and giggled.

"Wanna beer?" George asked. "Thersh about a gallon left. We gave it our bes' shot, but we couldn't finish it. Jus' couldn't get 'er done. Issa shame."

George drank the last four inches of beer from his tenth plastic cup. "An' thassa nuff, I think. Here's to Pinky Schroeder, the feaster of the found. I mean the founder of the feast."

Helen giggled again. "It's definitely time to quit," she said. "Any more and you'll start singing again, and I couldn't handle that at this time of the morning."

George stood up, stumbled, and then regained his balance. He tapped the ashes from his pipe into his palm and put the pipe in his shirt pocket.

"By the way, George, I shouldn't admit it, but that tobacco you were smoking really smelled good. Is it something new?" Helen asked.

"It's Half 'n' Half," said George. "Half Irish Flake and half reefer, otherwise known as marijuana, dope, grass, pot, weed, and prolly some other names of whish I am unaware."

Helen was shocked. "Where did you get it?"

"Off the ground. It was in an Irish Flake tin that somebody

dropped. But those tins are all over. I dunno who brought it, and I don't wanna know."

Helen laughed. "What does it do to you?"

"Nothing much. Makes you kind of mellow."

"That's one word for it," Helen said. "Put out the fire and come to bed."

George poured the water from the tub onto the embers and took Helen's arm.

"Better hold on so's you don' trip," he said. "It's darker 'n hell and you don' wanna trip."

"You're the one who's on a trip," Helen said, as they started up the hill together.

"Yup, I'm gathering buds."

"Drinking them, you mean."

"No, I mean rosebuds. 'Gather ye rosebuds while ye may, old time is still a-flying.' And so on. Robert Herrick. 'To the Virgins' from 1648."

"We don't qualify," said Helen.

The next morning, George woke up much later than usual, with a scratchy throat, a pounding sensation between the temples, and a mouth that tasted like the bottom of an owl's nest. It was his first hangover since October of 1982, when the Brewers lost to the Cardinals in the World Series. He sat up, groaned, and lay back down again. "I've either got to drink a lot more, or a lot less," he muttered. "I'm not used to this."

Helen came into the room and sat on the edge of the bed. "How are you feeling, George?" she asked, and gave him another one of those indulgent smiles.

"I feel like I've been peed on from a great height. I should have had more pizza."

"I'm sorry it was so bland," Helen said. "Emma gave me some fresh oregano for it, but I lost it somewhere, and all I could find in the cupboard was basil."

Thinking was painful under the circumstances, but it didn't take George long to figure out what had happened to the oregano.

"You lost it down by the campfire, and I smoked it. All of it. The world was spinning around, I thought it was reefer madness, like we used to read about, and all the time it was oregano and too much Budweiser. Maybe I should find a high school kid who'll sell me some of the real stuff."

George sat up and put his arm around Helen's shoulders. "You know, there are times when I think our life has been one long procession of dull moments, all work and no play. We were always the grown-ups while everybody else was drinking beer and smoking funny cigarettes and screwing around in general. Well, last night I took a trip back to the flaming youth I never had, and you can take it from me—there's a lot to be said for dull moments."

George spent a long time in the shower, and when he came into the kitchen for breakfast, he poured a tall glass of orange juice and drank it down in three swallows.

"Like Grandma Reilly used to say about Grandpa, 'I know himself doesn't drink at night, because he's always so thirsty in the morning.'"

Helen was sipping coffee and paging through George's copy of *Great Poems of the English Language.*

"I looked up Herrick," she said, "and found a couple of lines I really like."

> Come, let us go, while we are in our prime,
> And take the harmless folly of the time!

"That's far enough," said George. "From there on that poem gets kind of gloomy."

"Well, we can be gloomy some other day," Helen said. "I suppose our prime has come and gone, but are you in the mood for some harmless folly after breakfast?"

"What kind of folly have you got in mind?"

"Use your imagination."

"Oh. Well, I hate to disappoint you, Helen, but for the second time in our married life, I'm going to decline.

"I've got a headache."

Just a Gigolo

///

A damp and gusty wind slammed the door behind George as he came indoors.

"Well, Hans, it looks like the fall has come and gone. It's starting to rain, and the sky is getting pretty black to the southwest. Mark my words, by tonight it's going to turn into the first snow of the winter."

"I suppose we'd better head for home before it gets any worse," Hans said. He and his terrier, Ollie, had dropped by the lodge at the end of their morning walk.

A polite bark interrupted them. Russell had been swimming in the lake, and now he was sitting on the porch and asking to come in. George opened the door about an inch. "Russell, shake!" he commanded, and Russell shook himself from head to tail, rattling the tags on his collar and throwing water up, down, and sideways. Ollie met Russell at the door and the two dogs began to wrestle gently in front of the fireplace.

Hans was impressed. "Boy, I sure wish Ollie could learn to shake himself like that—before he comes in, rather than after. That frizzy coat of his soaks up a lot of rain, and if we don't dry him off he leaves a trail of water all over the house."

"Shaking off the water is part of Russell's training for duck hunting," explained George. "A big wet dog isn't an ideal companion in a small duck blind."

"Russell O'Malley, PhD," Hans said.

"Yeah, he's a smart one. He can trace his ancestors farther back than I can. A lot of his relatives are field champions, and his grandpa was a bona fide hero—he ran into a burning building once."

"To rescue a child?" Hans asked.

"No, there weren't any children, so he came back out with the fire insurance policy wrapped in a wet towel."

Helen gave George a disgusted look. "For God's sake, George, you know that never happened," she said.

"Maybe not," said George, with a wink at Hans, "but it makes a helluva story, and that's the important thing."

"Is there anything Russell doesn't know?" Hans asked.

"He's just starting to learn scent tracking," replied George. "For instance, if Helen is out for a walk and I can't see her, I'll give Russell one of her shoes to sniff and tell him to 'find Helen,' and most of the time he'll follow her scent trail until he locates her."

"Thanks a lot, George," Helen said. "Now Hans knows I have smelly feet."

"No more than anyone else," said George. "To a dog, any human foot must smell like a circus in August."

"You're getting in deeper, George," Helen warned. "Better quit while you can."

"I'll get out of here so you two can fight in peace," Hans said. "You're releasing built-up tensions, and that's a kind of cathartic self-treatment."

"If you walk home in the rain you'll need treatment for pneumonia," said George. "Hop in the truck and I'll give you a lift."

"OK, George, but first let me show you the trick I taught Ollie," Hans said. He took a thin brown dog treat from his shirt pocket.

"Ollie, sit!" he commanded. "Ollie, trust!" Hans laid the strip on Ollie's muzzle. "Trust . . . trust . . . trust . . ." Hans repeated. Ollie tried desperately to focus his eyes on the treat.

"OK!" said Hans, and Ollie flipped the strip into the air and caught it. George and Helen applauded. "What kind of a treat is that?" asked George. "Something new?"

"Yeah, it's called Dognip," Hans said. "They were giving samples away at the pet store in Green Bay, and Ollie will do anything for them. They're like canine cocaine."

When George got back, Helen was giving Russell a rubdown with an old bath towel. "I'll brush him while you change," she said. "You'll have to head over to the Rest in about half an hour."

The Rest was Rowley's Rest, an old resort hotel near Rowleys Bay that had been converted into a nursing home. Every Tuesday afternoon, George stopped by so the residents could play with Russell, who relished his role as an amateur therapy dog.

They usually started each visit with a group of fragile ladies George called the wallflowers. They had gentle, old-timey names like Violet, Grace, Eleanor, Rose, and Dorothy, and rarely left their beds. Russell sensed their infirmity and sat quietly at their bedsides, gravely offering a paw to be shaken and basking in the compliments that were lavished on him.

Next came the merry widows, a cadre of more rambunctious ladies who invited Russell into their beds and made ribald comments about how long it had been since they had shared a sheet with anything male.

And then there was the million-dollar infield, George's name for three ladies in wheelchairs who took turns throwing a tennis ball for Russell to fetch, down the hall in the winter and on the lawn in the summer. On this Tuesday they were in midseason form, and after a dozen retrieves the ball got soggy. George took out his handkerchief to dry it, but the ladies would have none of that.

"Don't bother!" said one of them. "We all grew up on farms, and we're used to really nasty stuff—calf snot and chicken manure and piglets with the scours. Dog spit is lemonade to us!"

At the Rest, old ladies outnumbered old men about ten to one, and the men tended to come and go, so George stopped to visit each of them. Russell always triggered a flood of reminiscences, and they would talk about the fabled cow-herding collies, legendary retrievers, and infallible rabbit chasers they had owned in their younger days.

George noticed that while some of the old gents told exactly the same stories every week, others made sweeping changes in their narratives, inventing new plots, cliff-hanger endings, and sometimes entirely new dogs. But he kept a straight face.

"What the hell," he said to himself. "I'm an Irish storyteller myself, and that's the worst kind. Most of my stories already have two or three coats of varnish, so who am I to criticize?"

The weather forecast had been correct; when George and Russell were ready to leave the Rest in the late afternoon, a blizzard was blowing in off the bay and the snow was already six inches deep.

At the front desk, Lois, the head nurse, bent down to pet Russell.

"Such a nice dog," she said. "Everybody loves him. He deserves some kind of reward for his efforts. Can I give him a treat?"

She took a Dognip from the pocket of her lab coat and held it out to Russell. He took it carefully from her fingers as he had been taught.

"What a gentleman he is," she remarked. "When I give one of these to my Airedale, Muggs, he almost takes my arm off at the elbow. But even so, Muggsy is a good dog. There isn't anything he wouldn't do for me, reward or no reward."

"Yeah," said George, "when you think about it, there isn't much of a percentage in being a dog. I mean, what do they get out of it? Russell will sit in a duck blind with me all day, and if I'm lucky enough to get a duck, he'll swim fifty yards in freezing water to fetch it, and when he does, all he gets from me is a pat on the head and a hearty 'well done.'"

"He does it for love, George—you know that as well as I do. So—we'll see you next Tuesday. So long, Russell."

It took George a half hour to drive home through the blinding snow, with the pickup in four-wheel drive and low range. When he and Russell came into the living room, Helen was sitting on one of the sofas, staring into the cold fireplace with some tissues in her hand. Russell jumped onto the sofa with her.

"Getting a cold, sweetheart?" George asked. "This is the season for it."

Helen turned to him and George could see she had been crying.

"No, I haven't got a cold," she said. "George, I've lost Great-grandma's ring."

"Oh no. The diamond ring?"

Helen nodded and began to cry again. Her great-grandmother Elsa Sorenson had worked for thirty-five years as a bookkeeper in a Saint Paul bank and was one of the first professional women of her generation in Minnesota. The ring had been a retirement present.

"Right after you left, the rain stopped for a while, so I hauled the last bag of mulch out to the rose beds in the wheelbarrow and spread it around while I still had a chance. That ring always was a little loose, and it must have come off . And by tomorrow there will be a foot of snow on top of it. I'll never find it, George. I just know I'll never find it!"

Russell looked into Helen's eyes and slowly wagged his tail. Helen leaned forward and hugged him. "Poor puppy," she said. "You know something is wrong, don't you? Well, it's not your fault if a stupid old lady wears a diamond ring while she's gardening."

Four decades of marriage had taught George that this wasn't the time to make helpful suggestions, so he put a hand on Helen's shoulder and said nothing.

It took Helen about a week to put the worst of the loss behind her, but as winter settled in George noticed that from time to time she would stare at her right hand and silently mourn the loss of Elsa Sorenson's diamond. Then she would spend hours probing the contents of drawers and cabinets and pockets.

The January thaw arrived on schedule during the last week of the month. The sun came out, the temperature jumped up into the fifties, and the Coot Lake Road gang went for a walk, ending up at the lodge, as usual. Helen, Emma, and Beth went down to the lake to talk about whatever women talk about, while George, Lloyd, Bump, and Hans sat on the south-facing porch steps, keeping an eye on the kids and dogs and soaking up the watery sunlight.

"How's Russell coming with his tracking?" Hans asked.

"Fair to middling," said George. "But isn't it time for a little competition, Russell versus Grits?"

None of Helen's shoes were handy, but a wicker basket holding her trowels, shears, pruning saws, and other gardening tools was just inside the door. George took a leather glove from the basket and let both dogs sniff it.

"Russell, find Helen!" George called out.

"Hunt'er up, Grits," Lloyd commanded.

Grits turned to the north, put his nose to the ground, picked up a scent, and took off, following the tracks the women had made in the melting snow. Russell faced the south wind. He wagged his tail furiously and loped down the driveway.

"Well, Russell's going real fast," said Lloyd, "but he's 180 degrees off course. Helen went north, and he's going south."

Russell stopped at one of the rose beds. He stuck his nose into the thin cover of snow that remained and began to dig in the woody mulch and black soil.

"Oh, for cripes sake," George said, and trilled a whistle to call Russell, who trotted back with something in his mouth. It was a leather glove. "Give," said George, and Russell dropped it. George put the glove into Helen's gardening basket with its mate.

"Not quite ready for prime time, are you, big puppy," George said, and rubbed Russell's ears. "Still, you smelled a glove and you fetched a glove." A few minutes later, the women appeared, led by Grits.

"Tracked you down, didn't he, Helen?" asked Lloyd. "There's no escape from Grits."

"Whenever I see Grits coming I feel like I've escaped from a chain gang in Mississippi," Emma remarked. "It was a relief to see he was after Helen."

On the first warm day in April, Helen pruned the rose bushes. She put on her leather gloves for protection from the thorns, and when she slipped on the right glove she felt her finger slide into a ring.

"It can't be!" she said, but it was. Great-grandma Elsa's diamond ring dropped out of the glove and sparkled in her palm.

"George!" she called. "George! You'll never guess . . ."

After hugs and kisses and general rejoicing, George told Helen about Russell's January thaw retrieve.

"Let me get this straight," Helen said. "I always wear that ring on my right hand, and when I took off my right glove that day in November, the ring stayed in it. And then I must have dropped one of the gloves in the flowerbed, but which glove, right or left? George, do you remember which glove Russell retrieved?"

"No, I didn't notice. But it doesn't really matter, does it?"

"Of course it does," said Helen. "If he dug up the glove with the ring in it he's a hero! But one thing is for sure—I'm going to get that ring appraised and insure it for whatever it's worth. And I'm not going to garden with rings on anymore."

The following Sunday morning, George drove to Baileys Harbor to buy the *New York Times*. It took a pot of coffee and an hour of steady reading to get through the heavy international stories. And then, at the bottom of page nineteen of the national news, he saw a headline that got his full attention.

Russell the Wonder Dog
Retriever Finds Heirloom Ring

By HARVEY DOWD

BAILEYS HARBOR, Wis.—A pedigreed golden retriever named Russell has found and returned a lost diamond ring worth $15,000.

The three-year-old dog is owned by Mr. and Mrs. George O'Malley, who live near Baileys Harbor in Door County, Wisconsin. Russell used the scent of a left-hand leather glove to find the right-hand glove of the pair, which was accidentally buried for two months in a flowerbed. And the right-hand glove contained the ring.

Mrs. O'Malley inherited the ring, set with a two-carat diamond, from her great-grandmother. Continued on Page A22 . . .

"Helen, look at this! You and Russell made the *Times*!"

"Wow, that was fast," Helen said. "I got the ring appraised, and then I called your friend Harvey in Chicago, and he wrote the story and said he would try to get it on the AP wire. That must be how the *Times* picked it up. We thought it would be a nice surprise."

"Well, I'm surprised, all right," said George. "But I don't understand the part about Russell finding the right-hand glove in January. We don't really know which glove he found."

"True," Helen admitted, and winked at George. "But it makes a better story this way, don't you think? Anyway, Russell is now getting his allotted fifteen minutes of fame, and he deserves a reward. Tomorrow I'll go into town and buy him a big bag of Dognips."

The next morning George was astounded to find that he had thirty-seven new e-mails. It took him two hours to read them all. "Most of them are from people I know, just kidding me," he said. "But Russell has a better reward than Dognips coming, Helen. One of the e-mails is from a golden retriever breeder in Escanaba, and he wants to know what Russell charges for his services."

Russell heard his name and wagged his tail. "Russell O'Malley, canine gigolo," said George. "Let's see, young man—you're twenty-one in dog years, and no offspring that I'm aware of, not even so much as a hot date. It's about time you were introduced to the facts of life.

"What do you think, Russell—are you up for a trip to Michigan? I've heard that those Youper girls really know how to show a fella a good time!"

Miracle on Coot Lake Road

George was pricing aged cheddar at the market in Baileys Harbor when a woman wearing a lot of perfume sneaked up behind him and tapped him on the shoulder.

"Hey, Georgie, do you still play your viola?" she asked. George turned to confront the source of the scent. It was Debbie Dombrowski, a jolly, flirtatious, and frequently married Door County native who had played the cello when George was a violist in the Sturgeon Bay high school orchestra, back in the long-gone 1950s.

"That's a helluva pickup line you've got there, Debbie," said George. "We've got to stop meeting like this—first at the class reunion and now at the cheese cooler. And the answer is yes and no. Can I still play? Sure. But do I still play? No, not much. I haven't had my viola out of the case for a month. There isn't much demand for it."

"Well, there is now. Limber up, Georgie—I need you," Debbie said.

"Be still, my heart!" George said. "Is that a proposition or a proposal?"

Debbie giggled and poked George in the chest with a forefinger.

"Georgie O'Malley, always kidding," she said. "Sorry to disappoint you, but right now it's your musical prowess I'm after. I know it's only October and the holidays are a long way off, but I thought it would be fun to put a string quartet together to play at the hospital and the old folks' homes on Christmas Eve. I'm going to call it the Accidental Quartet, and you could be our violist. It'll do wonders for your holiday spirit."

"Oh, I don't doubt it," said George. "After all, I'm practically an old folk myself. Who else is playing?"

"I'm playing cello, Cissy Sindelar is playing second violin, and the first violin is going to be a newcomer named David Samuel," Debbie said. "He lives in Sister Bay and just retired from the Chicago Symphony, so we'll have to be on our toes."

"Well, the viola part for 'Jingle Bells' was always within my reach. But do you think this virtuoso is going to tolerate a bunch of amateurs like you and Cissy and me?"

"I hope so," Debbie said. "He seems reasonably down-to-earth for a violinist, but wearing a Santa suit should bring him a little closer to our level. The plan is for you and David to be Santas, and Cissy and I will dress up like elves in green leotards with little short skirts. I'm going to rent the costumes in Green Bay."

"Say no more, Debbie—I'm a sucker for elves in short skirts," said George. "And the idea of playing 'Up on the Housetop' with a guy from the Chicago Symphony has a certain bizarre appeal. So you can count me in, Debbie, and we can come over to my place for coffee and cookies after our last gig. I'd like my grandson, Willie, to hear a quartet and see that I can do something besides fish for bluegills."

"Way to go, Georgie!" Debbie said. She hugged him and gave him a peck on the cheek. "I'll drop off your music and your costume, and the rehearsal will be at David's place on the twentieth of December."

"OK," George said. "But for God's sake, Debbie, let go of me. People will talk!"

Debbie took a quick look up and down the aisle. "No problem, Georgie, there aren't any people here, just tourists."

Back at the lodge, George told Helen about meeting Debbie in the market and agreeing to play in her quartet.

"Speaking of being in the market, did Debbie have anyone with her, like a man, for instance?" Helen asked. "At the beauty shop they were saying that her third divorce is final now and she's shopping around. Do you know of any eligible middle-aged men who would be interested in a middle-aged woman with season tickets for the Packers?"

"She's got season tickets?" George exclaimed. "If I'd known that, I would have married her myself."

"Very funny. Actually, she's only had them for a few years. They belonged to her second husband, and Debbie got them in the divorce settlement. They're supposed to be good seats, too. I wonder—does Lloyd Barnes like football?"

George drew himself up to his full height, what there was of it. "Helen, for the first time in our married life, I am going to insist on something. You will not play matchmaker again, and particularly not with anyone I know. Remember what happened the last time, when you tried to pair up Oscar and Betty?"

"Well, how was I supposed to know Oscar was gay?" Helen said. "He seemed like a nice, well-behaved man to me. What about this David Samuel—is he single?"

"Helen!"

"All right, all right. But getting back to Christmas, George—do you think Willie still believes in Santa? Every Christmas Eve since he was four, you've been dressing up in your dad's old Santa suit, but it's always been too big for you, and the moths have about finished it off. Willie will be eight this Christmas, and I'm not sure if we should keep up the pretense."

"Well," said George, "there are a few things men do that women generally don't. One of them is smoking a pipe and another is dressing up like Santa Claus. And a man can tell when he's got an unbeliever on his lap—there's something in the kid's tone of voice and the way he looks at your beard. I think Willie saw right through me last Christmas, and only went along with the whole Santa business because he knew we wanted him to. I'll impersonate Santa for Bump and Emma's kids—Mary is four and Brian is six, I think—but with Willie we'll have to play it by ear."

"Actually," Helen said, "if you're going to be gone most of Christmas Eve, Hans would be the ideal Santa. He's got the bowl full of jelly and a real white beard. I think I could patch up your dad's suit one more time, and let it out enough to fit, but first I'll talk to Beth. I'm not sure a retired shrink will play Santa. He might think it's traumatic or something."

After supper, George took his viola out of its case. It was a massive French instrument, with a body a full seventeen inches long. Although George was only five foot nine, he had big hands and long fingers that made it possible for him to play a viola that large. It had been his constant companion since he was twelve, when his fingers grew too big for the violin, and playing it in amateur string quartets and community orchestras had been his principal hobby during his years in Chicago. He tucked it under his chin and played the fifth Hoffmeister etude as far as he could remember it.

"Bravo," Helen said when he had finished.

"And they say size doesn't matter," said George. "When I was a kid I could barely play this monster, but I'm glad I kept it. A big, noisy viola is going to come in handy now that I've got to compete with a professional."

"But should you be competing with him?" Helen asked. "I thought you were supposed to blend."

"Don't you believe it," George said. "There's been a war between the violins and the violas for more than three hundred years. The first fiddles get all the interesting parts, so we violas try to drown them out when we get a chance."

"I swear I'll never understand string players," said Helen with a sigh. "You can make the most beautiful sounds, but when you're not arguing with conductors about bowings, you're fighting with each other."

"Don't get me started on conductors," warned George. "Most of them are just pianists that didn't make the grade."

The Accidental Quartet's first and only rehearsal went well. As they expected, David Samuel was a stellar violinist, but he was also genial and funny and accepted the idea of wearing a Santa costume with good grace. "I tried it on and it fits," he said, "but I may take a few liberties with it. I must say, though, that wearing that red suit gave me a strange sense of power. One minute I was Dave Samuel, mild-mannered violinist, and the next I was Super Santa, faster than a speeding bullet and able to leap tall buildings at a single bound."

"I've had that same feeling," George said. "If you're not careful, you become drunk with power. 'You better watch out, I'm making a list, I know if you've been bad or good.' And you start referring to yourself in the third person, like royalty. Creepy."

When they took a break, Samuel's wife, Hannah, showed them around the house, which had a spectacular view of the bay. But George noticed something that made him wonder. When the rehearsal was over and they walked to their cars, George drew Debbie aside.

"Did you notice they didn't have a Christmas tree?" he asked. "And did you look at the mantelpiece?"

"I sure did," Debbie said. "Isn't that a beautiful candelabra?"

"It isn't a candelabra, it's a menorah," said George. "And most of those cards on the mantel were Hanukkah cards. I don't know how you did it, Debbie, but you talked a Jewish violinist into wearing a Santa suit and playing carols for a lot of elderly Gentiles on Christmas Eve!"

"Oh my God," Debbie said. "I never gave it a thought."

"One thing's for sure," George said. "He's got a sense of humor."

When George got home from the rehearsal, Helen was bursting with news.

"I hardly know where to start," she said. "First of all, you won't have to play Santa for the kids on Christmas Eve, because Hans has agreed to do it. Beth said he tried on your dad's old Santa suit, and he's perfect for the part. He thinks kids should have a rich fantasy life, so believing in Santa is a good thing, as far as he is concerned. But the real news is pretty spectacular—I found out what happened to Debbie's first marriage!"

"Helen . . . ," George began, with a warning note in his voice.

"Just hear me out, George," said Helen. "When I was getting my hair done this afternoon, LaVerne told me all about it, and she got it straight from Debbie. It turns out that Debbie's first husband was named Donnie Dombrowski, and he was a plumber from Sturgeon

Bay. Debbie was living in Sturgeon Bay at the time, and she met him when he came to her apartment to replace a leaky water heater.

"It was a hot day and Donnie just had jeans and a T-shirt on, and apparently Debbie was pretty impressed with his biceps and things when he carried the old heater out and the new one in, all by himself. So they started seeing each other, and they were married within a couple of months.

"Well, Debbie was a big Packers fan even then, and her prize possession was a genuine league football autographed by the 1966 Packers—Vince Lombardi, Bart Starr, Paul Hornung, and the whole gang. But when the honeymoon was over she discovered that Donnie had a dirty little secret—he was originally from Chicago and he was a die-hard Bears fan."

"Oh, brother," George said.

"It gets worse," Helen went on. "After they had been married about a year, Donnie got a chance to buy an autographed Dick Butkus game jersey, so he sold Debbie's football to raise enough money to buy the jersey—and never told Debbie. When she found out, she was so mad she divorced him. Well, according to LaVerne, Debbie has forgiven him, she uses his name whenever she isn't married to someone else, and she still dreams about his biceps, but it's too late. Isn't that sad?"

"Talk about a rich fantasy life," said George. "It's like something on afternoon television."

The remaining three days before Christmas Eve were filled with activity. George found a suitable spruce on the edge of the swamp, brought it home, and trimmed it. Bill, Josie, and Willie arrived from Chicago, and the lodge was filled with the aromas of buttermilk, anise, pecans, and dates as Norwegian Christmas cookies came out of the oven. George was gone half of the time, on last-minute shopping trips. He noticed that whenever he got home, Helen was on the Internet or talking quietly on the telephone. Something was afoot, but it was Christmas, and he decided not to inquire.

The Accidental Quartet assembled at the lodge about five o'clock in the afternoon of Christmas Eve. They put their instruments and music stands in the back of Helen's Buick station wagon and made the rounds of the hospital and the retirement and nursing homes, starting in Sturgeon Bay and working their way north. Their performances went smoothly, and they were on schedule until they got to Sister Bay, where they arrived minutes after a giant Lutheran choir descended on the village like raiding Vikings. The choir used up all the convenient parking places, and the Accidentals had to lug their cases and stands five blocks through the snow.

"I never realized they let singers drive cars, just like real musicians," George said loudly, as they trudged along behind a gaggle of matronly altos.

"Shut up, O'Malley," one of the women replied, without turning around. "If I played a viola I wouldn't let on."

"Sylvia Nielson, is that you?" George asked. "I'd recognize your voice anywhere—you sound just like Louis Armstrong."

As they were leaving their last gig, Debbie took a close look at David.

"You talked about taking some liberties with your Santa suit, but I don't see any," she said.

"Actually," David replied, "I was thinking of wearing a yarmulke, just to be ecumenical, but at the last minute I changed my mind. I thought it might confuse the old dears."

George got behind the wheel of the Buick, and they headed for Coot Lake Road through a light snow. "I don't know about you guys, but this evening was the highlight of my Christmas so far," he said. "I can't think of anything I would rather do than drive around Door County on Christmas Eve with a string quartet. Why don't we make the Accidentals intentional and permanent?"

"Motion carried," they all said.

When they arrived at the lodge, Willie, Brian, and Mary were taking turns sitting on the lap of Santa Hans, and the kids were surprised when two more Santas carrying instrument cases came into the living room.

Helen was quick to explain. "That's the real Santa, kids," she said, pointing to Hans, "and these are his helpers, and these are his elves." Willie and Brian exchanged cynical glances, and even four-year-old Mary looked suspicious. But they brightened up when the helpers and the elves took out their instruments and played "All I Want for Christmas Is My Two Front Teeth" for them. Musical Santas were something new.

"OK, everybody, time to get in line for cookies and coffee cake," Helen said when the music ended. "Everything is in the kitchen."

George was first in line, and when he came back into the living room with his plate, he was surprised to see yet another Santa sitting on one of the sofas by the fireplace. He looked back; sure enough, Hans and David were still in the kitchen.

"One, two, and I make three—where the hell did the fourth one come from?" he thought. Debbie was behind George, and she was even more curious. The fourth Santa took her hands in his and laughed in a deep bass voice.

"Ho, ho, ho! What's your name, little girl?"

"Debbie."

"Well, Debbie, sit on Santa's lap and tell him what you want for Christmas."

Debbie giggled. "OK, but keep your hands to yourself."

"Have you been a good girl this year?"

"That depends. Anyway, it's none of your business," Debbie said.

"Ho, ho, ho! I'm sure you've been good—Santa has a way of knowing these things. Santa knows what you want for Christmas, too." He took a gaily wrapped package from behind the sofa and handed it to her.

"I can't believe it," said Debbie. "You sound just like my first husband."

"That's because I am your first husband," he said, and pulled off his false beard.

"Donnie!"

"Go ahead, open your present," said Donnie. Debbie tore off the paper. It was her 1966 autographed Packers football.

There was a certain amount of embracing and murmuring.

Willie and Brian stared, sniggered, and made kissing noises until their parents dragged them back into the kitchen.

"I've got tickets for the Packers' playoff game with the Bears next week," Debbie whispered. "You want to go, Donnie?"

"You bet," Donnie said. "Go, Pack, Go!" But then he turned away and stuck out his tongue.

About a half hour later, Bill and Josie and Willie had gone to bed, and everyone but Hans and Beth had left. They were sitting at the kitchen table with George and Helen, having a final cup of coffee.

"Thanks for being Santa, Hans," Helen said. "Was it fun?"

"By and large, but next time, Helen, don't let the kids watch *Miracle on 34th Street* right before I arrive. They kept pulling on my beard to see if it was real, and dammit, it is!"

"Apart from that, though, I'm the one who should be thanking you," said Hans. "Putting on that costume and playing the Santa role gave me the idea for a whole new branch of psychotherapy. I'm going to call it Primal Santa."

"Oh no," Beth said. "He's going to be funny. Helen, how do you deal with George when he's funny?"

"I laugh," Helen replied. "All in all, it's the quickest way to get it over with."

"No, I'm serious," said Hans. "Who is Santa but a friendly fat man with a big beard who listens to all your hopes and dreams and tells you that you've been good? Well, I did that for thirty years, except that instead of a lap I had a couch, and I wore a tweed jacket with leather patches on the elbows instead of a red suit with fur trim. But the principle is the same."

Hans glanced at Beth. "And I'm going to field-test it immediately, starting with that red-headed waitress at the Sandpiper. She's probably riddled with inhibitions that I can cure."

"Don't even think about it," Beth warned.

"It's a joke, Beth," Hans said. "Hey, George, have you ever noticed that Norwegian women never seem to know when you're kidding?"

"It's the bane of my existence," said George.

After the Berges had left, George turned out the lights. He and Helen sat on one of the sofas in front of the fireplace and looked at the Christmas tree.

"To think that Donnie and Debbie are back together again after all these years," Helen said. "Isn't it romantic?"

"Matchmaker, matchmaker," said George. "How in the world did you manage it?"

"It wasn't easy. In fact, it was kind of a miracle. You have no idea how many plumbers named Dombrowski there are in the Midwest, but I finally found Donnie on the north side of Chicago. Then Donnie found the man who had bought the football from him, and that man still had it and was willing to sell it, which was another miracle. God knows what Donnie had to pay for it. And finally he rented a Santa suit and drove all the way up here on Christmas Eve. Looks like 100 percent true love to me!"

"Let's say 99 percent," George said. "You didn't see the face he made after he said, 'Go, Pack, Go.'"

"But they left together and Debbie forgot her cello. That must mean something. And speaking of which, how did your musical tour of Door County go tonight?"

"It was wonderful, Helen. We gave away a lot of smiles tonight. I can still see those happy, wrinkled old faces, and that reminded me that before long, we'll be the wrinkled ones. Not you, Helen, of course."

"Of course," said Helen. "But seriously, George, everybody says that it's better to give than to receive, and every Christmas you find out it's true. By the way, what do you want for Christmas, George?"

"Well, I would like one of those sixty-inch TVs, but I'll settle for a kiss."

"Coming right up," Helen said.

"As soon as you ditch the whiskers."

Petter Takes the Plunge

///

*O*n a cold, gray afternoon in early December, George was tying flies. He secured the nose of a completed number ten Golden Parachute with a whip finish and applied a few drops of glue to the yellow thread that held the body, wing, and hackle on the hook. While the glue dried, he assembled the tiny quantities of calf hair and yellow chicken hackle he would need to tie another. The Golden Parachute was a high-floating, soft-landing, bluegill-catching dry fly that he had invented, and it was so effective that George kept it secret.

Helen had walked out to the road to get the mail. When she returned, George was inspecting the new Parachute with a magnifying glass. "Another triumph," he said. "If the lake wasn't frozen over, I'd go out and try it. But it's hard to cast a fly into those little ice-fishing holes."

Helen had heard that one before. She stamped her feet to knock the snow off her boots and waited a minute for the condensation to clear from her glasses.

"This is all we got, and it looks like the first Christmas card of the season," she said, holding an envelope up to the fading light from the south windows. "Who do we know in North Dakota? I can barely make out the return address, but there's a Grand Forks postmark."

"Don't look at me," said George. "In North Dakota, the Irish are about as scarce as shamrocks. It must be from some Norwegian relative of yours."

Helen opened the envelope and took out a card and letter. "You're right, George, it's from Aunt Signe Sorenson, but I thought she lived in Thief River Falls."

Dear Helen,

I don't know if you remember me, but I was your Uncle Lars Solberg's half sister. Well, I still am, but he's dead. That makes me your half aunt, I guess. Anyways, you might remember visiting us in Minnesota when you were a little girl. I was married to Soren then—Soren Sorenson—but one time in 1952 he went ice fishing on Leech Lake and never came back. He must have fell through the ice. I waited the better part of two years, but he never showed up, so I married Petter Sorenson, no relation to Soren, and we moved to Grand Forks.

We like it here but we're both 83 and I don't put up with the cold like I used to. So we were thinking about going south for the winter, and we wondered if it would be OK if we stayed by you for a couple of days? Actually it would be the last two days in December and the first two days in January. Because Petter has read about the Polar Bear Plunge by you there in Jacksonport, where they jump into Lake Michigan on New Year's Day and freeze their particulars off, and he wants to try it once before he dies.

I tell him at his age it might be the last thing he ever does, and he says so what. So anyways, Helen, please write or call and let us know if we could come by. We wouldn't be much trouble, just a couple of old Norwegians, and if you like I could show you how to make lefse and krumkake.

So yrs. truly,
Aunt Signe

(Petter don't talk much but he says ya)

Helen took off her glasses and wiped them with the hem of her sweater. "Those dear old people," she said. "You wouldn't mind if I invited them, would you, George?"

"Go ahead," George replied. "Petter sounds like a good listener and a man of few words. But I warn you, Helen, I am not going to strip off and hold his hand while he immerses his eighty-three-year-old body in thirty-one-degree water. I'll watch, and I'll send flowers to his funeral, but that's as far as I'll go."

Christmas came and went quite merrily, with its highlight a three-day visit from Bill, Josie, and Willie. But no sooner had they left than Helen started a second midwinter round of housecleaning. "You just help me strip the beds and wax the floors, George, and you can get back to your Trollope and fly-tying. I'll do the rest. I wouldn't want Signe to think I keep a sloppy house."

George was on the porch filling the bird feeders when Petter and Signe arrived, late in the afternoon of December 30. Petter was driving a very old Saab very slowly, and as he inched closer George could see that he was holding up a sheet of paper that almost completely blocked his view ahead.

George waved his arms. "Stop!" he yelled, and Petter braked gently to a halt about a foot from the tailgate of George's pickup. Petter got out of the car and shook George's hand while Helen hugged Signe.

"Ya, this was a good map you sent us," said Petter, folding the paper and sticking it in his shirt pocket. "My son, he loaned me a GPS for this trip, but when we got to Bemidji I shut the damn thing off. Couldn't stand that woman telling me what to do all the time. I get enough of that as it is.

"But shee! I'm glad I brought some extra money on account of we had a little car trouble in Fergus Falls, but it was just a bad fuel pump. I told Signe, I said, we should never have bought a Swedish car, but the Norwegians don't build any. And crumps, them motels charge an arm and a leg. The one in Chippewa Falls wanted sixty bucks, and the bed was about ten feet wide. I told Signe, for that kind of money they should provide another woman to help warm it up.

"Ya, the older you get the less fun it is to travel, but I told Signe, when we're on the road I can eat lemon meringue pie three meals a day if I want to, and that makes up for a lot."

Petter continued to talk in the empty living room as George and Helen and Signe carried suitcases into the lodge and upstairs to the spare bedroom.

"Petter don't say much, eh?" George whispered. "Apparently he's only a man of few words when Signe is talking."

After breakfast on the thirty-first, Helen and Signe peeled and boiled and riced a bag of potatoes and baked lefse on a steel griddle that George had made to fit the top of the stove. Helen baked two dozen lefse following the recipe her mother had taught her, and Signe made two dozen the way her mother had done it. When they were finished they exchanged recipes, but in later years, neither woman ever used the other woman's recipe. "Too much lard," said Helen. "Not enough lard," said Signe.

For lunch, they ate cranberry sauce and leftover dark meat from the Christmas turkey, rolled up in lefse. "George doesn't like lutefisk," Helen said, "so we use up the lefse and the dark meat this way. He calls these Norwegian tacos."

"Ya, lutefisk is strong stuff," said Petter. "I tell Signe, ya, the lutefisk eats a hole in your stomach, and the lefse is the patch."

After they had eaten, Helen got out the family Bible and her mother's scrapbooks, and she and Signe started drawing up a family tree.

"We'll be at this all afternoon, George," Helen said. "Why don't you take Petter for a drive and show him the sights?"

George's first stop was the Washington Island ferry dock at Northport. They watched the ferry breaking ice on its way into the landing and looked at rafts of mergansers that were swimming in patches of open water.

"Ya," said Petter as he focused the binoculars George had handed him. "Pa and I used to hunt them sawbills on the Red River. What did you call 'em—mergansers?"

"Did you ever eat a merganser?" George asked.

"Ya, sure," Petter said. "They tasted like lutefisk. And shee! they was tough. A very durable duck, Pa used to say."

On the way back to Coot Lake, they stopped for coffee at Al Johnson's Swedish Restaurant in Sister Bay. "Too bad it's the middle of winter," said George. "They've got sod on the roof of this building, just like in the old country, and in the summer a family of goats lives up there."

"Ya, the Swedes do goofy stuff," Petter said, and began to sing: "A t'ousand Swedes ran through the weeds, pursued by one Norwegian, we all took snuff, but it wasn't enough, in the battle of Copenhagen.

"Speaking of which, George, have you got any snoose? Signe, she don't let me use it no more."

"Nope. Pipe tobacco, but no snoose."

"Lemme see it," said Petter. He opened George's tobacco pouch, pulled out a chunk of Irish Flake, and tucked it into his cheek. "Mild," he said.

After supper, Petter looked at George's fly-tying bench and watched him make another Golden Parachute.

"Ya, Pa he used to fish for trout, but he used blasting powder. He could get twenty trout at a time that way—called it his DuPont fly rod," Petter said.

Later that evening, George looked up the Jacksonport Polar Bear Plunge on the Internet and printed out a legal document.

"First off, Petter," he said, "you have to sign this waiver of rights that says you understand the risks, hazards, and dangers of jumping into Lake Michigan in January."

"Like what?" Petter asked.

"Like sudden changes in temperature that can lead to loss of consciousness, hypothermia, heart attacks, and other life-threatening conditions, it says here."

"What's hypothermia mean?" Petter asked.

"It means getting really cold," replied George.

"Ho! I been cold lots of times. Where do I sign?"

"There's some other advice," George said, looking at the website. "Let's see: get there early so you can find a place to park, wear sneakers so you don't cut your feet on the ice, have some dry socks for when you get out of the water, bring a blanket to sit on, and don't wear your glasses because if they fall off you'll never find them."

"Ya, sounds good," said Petter.

George, Helen, Signe, and Petter left the lodge at about ten in the morning on New Year's Day and drove to Jacksonport in Helen's old Buick wagon. When they got there, it was obvious that everyone else had read and followed the advice about being early—cars were bumper to bumper as much as a quarter mile away from the park on the lakeshore that was the site of the plunge, and hundreds of people in various stages of undress were clogging the streets of the little town.

"Ya, I wonder who are the biggest damn fools—the ones that are going to yump in the lake, or the ones who come to watch," Petter remarked.

By the time they found a place to leave the car and walked to the park it was after eleven. "Ladies," George said, "you had better wait for Petter and me right here by the highway—otherwise we'll get separated. Come on, Petter, the plungers are supposed to assemble down by the lake."

George and Petter walked to the beach and handed in the waiver agreement. "I'll stay here and hang onto your clothes and your glasses and your blanket, so look for me when you get out of the water," George said.

"Ya," said Petter, "but I dunno, George, I wasn't really thinking that there would be so many women here. All I got on underneath is my Fruit of the Looms."

"Well, I wouldn't worry, Petter. Most of the women are wearing less than that. Just make sure they stay hitched up. The elastic could stretch in the cold."

When Petter was stripped down to his boxers, George was surprised to see how muscular he was for his age. But what astounded him more was the faded tattoo of a full-rigged ship that covered most of Petter's back.

"Jesus, Petter, where did you get the artwork?"

"In Hong Kong, when I was in the navy. I don't know how it happened, but I went ashore and the next morning, ya, there it was."

"Is everybody ready?" bellowed a voice through a bullhorn. "Five, four, three, two, one—go!"

There was an outburst of shrieks and yells that sounded like Pickett's Charge at Gettysburg. About a thousand pink, jiggling people ran past Petter and George. Petter hesitated until a lithe young blonde woman in a black Speedo grabbed him by the hand and dragged him into the horde of swimmers.

Within minutes the horde had had enough and ran back ashore, shaking the water out of their hair and slapping themselves to restore circulation. But there was no sign of Petter, and George began to worry.

"He didn't have his glasses on—maybe he didn't see me," George thought, and started walking toward the highway. Deputy Doug's black sheriff's patrol car was parked nearby, and as George approached it he saw that Helen and Signe were laughing and talking to Doug.

"Doug, we've got a missing person," said George. "A man about six feet, in his eighties, gray hair, white boxer shorts, and a big ship tattooed on his back."

"Who is that?" Signe asked.

"Petter," George said. "I saw him headed for the lake, but I didn't see him come back."

"But Petter doesn't have a ship on his back!" Signe said.

"Oh, yes, he does," said George. "I just saw it twenty minutes ago."

"George, Signe ought to know if her husband has a tattoo or not!" Helen said.

Signe covered her mouth with her hand and giggled. "Well, I've got to admit, I'm not sure what's on his back. Petter is kind of modest, and it's only been the last few years that we've even got undressed with the lights on."

Helen had been scanning the crowd for Petter. She tapped George on the shoulder. "Look over by the picnic shelter," she whispered. "Do you see what I see?"

It was Petter in his wet underwear, apparently unaffected by the cold and standing very close to the blonde in the black Speedo. She held his hand and then enveloped him in a hug while a young man snapped pictures. Then she gave him a kiss, waved, and walked off with the young man.

"Petter!" George shouted.

"Oh, good, have you found him, George?" Signe asked. "I've got my old glasses on and I can't see very far."

When Petter was toweled off and dressed, George took him to one side. "Looks like you got lucky, Petter!"

"Ya, a little, anyhow. I was damn cold, but what the hey, you're only young once. She was cold, too, so I was kind of a windbreak," Petter said. "She liked my tattoo, and she said I was pretty neat to be yumping in the lake at my age. Is it good when a young woman says you're neat, George?"

"It is if your wife isn't around," George replied.

The next morning Signe and Petter got up early, packed the old Saab, and came back indoors for breakfast. Helen poured mugs of coffee and handed out plates of krumkake.

When the krumkake was gone, Petter put on his jacket and headed for the door.

"What's your next stop, Petter?" George asked.

"Oh, I figger if we get a wiggle on, we can get back to Chippewa Falls by suppertime," Petter replied.

"Chippewa Falls? I thought you were going south for the winter," George said.

"We did," said Petter. "This was it. Ya, the TV said it was fifteen below every night in Grand Forks. It was a lot warmer here."

Petter's voice dropped to a whisper. "And besides, George," he said, "that young fella is going to send me the pictures he took. So I got to get back right away and show them around at the Sons of Norway and the barbershop.

"Shee! I never knew how good a woman looks in a tight black bathing suit like that. I wonder if they got 'em in Signe's size? Well, probably not. But I bet they have some that'll fit Helen. You oughta check, George. Pa, he used to say, you only go around once.

"Anyhow, thanks, George. I had a real good time, and we'll be back next year. Ya, ya, you're as young as you feel. Happy New Year!"

After Signe and Petter drove away, Helen brought in mugs of fresh coffee. "What were you and Petter whispering about?" she asked.

"I'll never tell," replied George. "But I'll give you a hint: what size swimsuit do you wear?"

"I haven't the foggiest," Helen said. "Why do you . . ." She stopped in midsentence and glared at George.

"George Thomas O'Malley, I am not going to freeze my particulars off in Lake Michigan with Petter next year. Or with you, either!"

"No, no," George said. "Nothing like that. I have something a lot warmer in mind.

"Helen, what do you say we put in a sauna?"

Hidden Depths

On a Friday night in mid-October, the members of the Baileys Harbor Bird and Booyah Club were sitting at a table in Snuffy O'Toole's Tavern, sipping draft Guinness and watching the seventh and final game of the World Series on Snuffy's big-screen TV. The married members had been exiled from their homes by their wives, who wanted to watch an episode of *The Fattest Loser* that aired at the same time as the series.

George had spent the better part of the afternoon trying to convince Helen that their cable hookup allowed them to watch two shows and record a third one at the same time.

"It's simple, Helen," he said. "You just . . ."

But Helen had interrupted. "I know you think it's simple, George, but if we pushed the wrong button we could miss everything. You boys just go to Snuffy's and let us do it our way. I don't know why you want to watch another baseball game, anyway. You've been watching baseball since April."

In the bottom of the third, the American League pitcher struck out the side and a long commercial break began. George signaled Snuffy to bring another round.

"You know, I'm not sure how much of a blessing cable TV really is," said Hans. "We've got all those channels, but tonight we had to go to a bar to watch the ball game, just like they did in 1950. And I don't think much of paying to watch commercials, either. Just the other night I made myself a little snack, turned on the TV to watch a movie, and I had to sit through five minutes of colon health and bloating. It put me right off my crackers and Cheez Whiz. I wound up watching the battle of the bulge on the Hitler channel."

"Bloating is bad, but ED is worse," George said. "Why don't they just say what they mean instead of hinting around about being 'ready'?"

"You said it, George," Bump replied. "And the situations in those commercials are so phony. The husband and wife are painting the kitchen, she bumps into him, he gives her a look, and all of a sudden it's passion city. Lemme tell ya, it ain't that easy to get things started after you've put in a ten-hour day pumping septic tanks in cold weather. And every time I see that commercial I wonder—do they stop to clean their brushes first, or do they just go for it?

"But the absolute pits is when you're watching TV with your wife and they tell you to see a doctor if you have a—condition— that lasts longer than four hours. Jeez, the first time Emma heard that she laughed so loud she woke up the kids."

"And then there's the one where the man and the woman are sitting in claw-footed bathtubs, out in the cold and naked as jaybirds," George said. "What are they thinking? For one thing, those old cast-iron tubs are cold on the backside—no wonder they can't get going. And any fool can tell you, not much is going to happen until you're both in the same tub. That's the one where you're supposed to 'see Alice.' I don't know who Alice is, but she must be hot stuff. Get it?"

They all stared straight ahead. "It's a joke, guys," explained George.

"And a jolly good one, too," Hans said. The commercial break ended, and the Baileys Harbor boys resumed watching the game. The first batter worked a 3–2 count, and the pitcher stepped off the mound. The tension built.

And then a tall, bulky, and commanding woman swept into the bar. "Oh God, it's Lucy," Snuffy whispered. "Man your battle stations."

The woman sat down at their table and handed a brochure to each of the men. "My name is Schmitz and I'm running for the school board," she said, "on a platform of lower taxes and better education."

"That ought to be popular," said Hans. "How do you propose to do it?"

"With more computers and less frills," she answered.

"You mean *fewer* frills," George said. "What kind of frills would you cut? Not English, I hope."

"The egghead stuff and foreign languages. And we can do without orchestra and longhair music. Our students need practical experience to get them ready for the real world."

"Oh, now you are venturing into deep waters," cautioned Hans. "What is the real world? Plato said that the things we perceive are only shadows . . ."

"Plato never had to meet a payroll," the woman said, and scowled at Hans. "Don't forget to vote in April." She took a stack of her brochures out of a shoulder bag, put them on the bar, and left.

"Who the hell was that, Snuffy?" George asked.

"That," said Snuffy, "was Lucinda Schmitz. And that was her idea of campaigning. About once a week she comes in, practically threatens my customers, and leaves a pile of literature. I just throw it away."

"Where does she stand politically?" George asked. "To the right of center, I presume?"

"To the right of North Korea," Snuffy said. "She and her husband own a computer store. I can't prove it, but I suspect she's running for the school board because she wants to sell computers and software to the schools."

The next morning, George sat at the kitchen table with a pad and pencil and read Lucinda's brochure from front to back, smoking his pipe and taking notes.

"Well, Helen," said George, "after you discard all the boilerplate about stuff that will never happen, like cutting taxes and creating jobs, her platform boils down to dumping the arts, the humanities, and the sports that lose money, and spending the savings on computers and business courses. If she had her way the curriculum would consist of computers, accounting, and football, I guess. But it's a free country, and any idiot can run for office."

"Such as you, for instance," Helen said.

George coughed and blew a cloud of fine gray ash out of the bowl of his pipe.

"You're kidding," he said.

"No," Helen replied. "I'm serious. Rita Carlson resigned from the board, and her seat will be open in April. So far Lucinda is the only declared candidate. So if nobody else runs, all Lucinda needs is to vote for herself and she'll get the seat. But you could beat her, George. You have hidden depths. You also have lots of spare time."

"Flattery will get you nowhere," said George. "Have you ever seen Lucinda? She outweighs me by a hundred pounds, and it's all muscle. If I tangled with her, I wouldn't last two minutes."

"I don't think you will have to wrestle with her, George, but if you do, you will make a handsome corpse. Just think about it, OK?"

George mulled the proposition over for a week. He had planned a restful, quiet winter of reading, writing, and fly-tying, but he shuddered when he thought of Lucinda creating a conservative majority on the board. In the end he decided to take a stab at public office.

He declared his candidacy, filed the required financial forms, and circulated nomination papers. He was gratified to see how quickly the papers accumulated signatures, and before long he was officially a candidate for the Northern Door School Board.

In mid-November, the Coot Lake political machine met for the first time. It consisted of George's neighbors and Snuffy. Snuffy knew politics as only an Irish saloonkeeper can know them, and his bar was the most important public forum in the northern half of the peninsula.

"You're a Democrat, George, so you'll get the liberals and some of the independents," Snuffy said. "Lucinda will get all the knee-jerk righties and the rest of the independents. But if you're reasonable and moderate you could come in slightly ahead of Lucinda. Do you think you could be reasonable and moderate, George?"

"I've never tried it, but I suppose it's worth a shot," replied George.

Winter campaigning in northern Door County was easier than George had expected, because at that time of year practically every adult he met was a year-round resident and a registered voter. He held forth at Snuffy's, the barbershop, and various markets at least once a week, and spent the rest of his time canvassing and dropping literature door to door.

Helen usually accompanied him, and she was a born campaigner; she seemed to know everyone and had an indelible memory for names. One day they knocked at the door of a three-story limestone palace with a copper roof, and discovered it was the home of Tess Underwood, Door County's richest and most devastatingly upper-class Democrat. She invited them in for a cup of coffee, and when it was time to leave, she hugged Helen warmly.

"You're sure to win, my dear, and I'll be glad to work on your campaign," she said.

Helen laughed. "Oh, no, Mrs. Underwood, my husband is the candidate. I'm just helping out."

Mrs. Underwood turned slowly and looked George up and down. "Pity," she said.

When Helen was busy elsewhere, George brought Russell along and put him on a sit and stay before knocking on doors.

"Hello, my name is George O'Malley and I am running for the school board in April," he would say, only to be interrupted by voters who were more interested in Russell.

"What a nice dog. Look, kids, isn't he beautiful? What's his name? He doesn't even move! How did you train him to sit like that?"

After a while, George heard through the grapevine that he was becoming known as the candidate with the golden retriever and the good-looking wife, but he didn't care; a vote was a vote.

One afternoon in early March, George pulled in to the lodge's driveway at the same time Helen was pulling out. They stopped and rolled their windows down.

"We've got to stop meeting like this, George, but Tess Underwood has invited me for tea," Helen said. "She's having a few friends in, and it's pretty much a command performance. Took me most of the day to get all dolled up. Warm up the leftover spaghetti, and I'll be home eventually."

"Leftover spaghetti again?" George said. "Dammit, I wish I'd never gotten into politics."

Helen shot him a sympathetic look. "I know, I know—but it won't be long now, sweetheart. Gotta go!"

The message light on the telephone was blinking when George went into the kitchen. There were a dozen messages, all for Helen; eleven from women and one from a man named Nils.

"Your boyfriend called while you were hobnobbing with the rich and famous," George said when Helen returned from the Underwoods at about midnight. "Nils, he said his name was. Who is Nils?"

"Nils Nilsson, and don't get jealous, he's twice your age."

"Helen, no one is twice my age. It's physically impossible to be twice my age."

"Oh, you know what I mean—he's old. And married. Like us."

"Sorry, Helen," said George. "It's been a long day. But tell me—what did you do at this eight-hour hen party *chez* Underwood?"

"It was a political meeting, and it took that long to flesh out plan B. Oh, dammit, I wasn't supposed to mention that quite yet—but listen, George, if we're going to win this election we might need a fallback position, and that's plan B. It's a version of 'good cop, bad cop,' but with two good cops. Here's how it will work . . ."

The Coot Lake political machine couldn't afford to conduct a poll, but Snuffy listened carefully to the political arguments in his bar, and the barber in Baileys Harbor monitored the endless talk among waiting customers. In late March, Snuffy was pessimistic. "We're falling behind, George, but we still have a chance. It's time to get ready for the debate."

George got cold feet whenever he was reminded of the debate. The Door County Women's League had scheduled it on the Tuesday night a week before the election, and George was worried.

"Just keep your cool," Snuffy said. "Don't take any extreme positions; in fact, don't commit yourself to much of anything. Give 'em the old blarney about lowering their taxes, and don't let Lucinda get your goat. If I know Lucinda, that will tick her off and she'll make a fool of herself."

Lucinda's campaign could afford a poll, and in late March it showed her ahead by ten points with a five-point margin of error. As soon as the numbers were crunched, Lucinda got a call from a political operative in Madison.

"That little Irishman is like an old racehorse," the operative said. "He'll start fast and fade in the stretch. Call him a liberal and a big spender, and promise to lower the school tax levy—voters always fall for that."

The night of the debate was cold and windy, and low clouds were spitting a little snow as George and Helen drove to Gibraltar High School. But the auditorium was full to overflowing, and the janitors were busy bringing in more chairs. Two lecterns were set up on the stage.

"I don't know, Helen," said George. "Snuffy wants me to be reasonable and moderate and say nothing but platitudes, but whenever I try that in front of a mirror I look like a liar and probably sound like one, too. People have a right to know where I stand. I feel some eloquence coming on."

"Follow your conscience," Helen said. "If we need it, we'll fall back on plan B. Oops, here comes Snuffy."

"'I've seen Lucinda speak," said Snuffy. "She reads everything from index cards and likes to hide behind the lectern. So you should do the opposite—walk around and don't use your notes."

Betty Swain, a formidable retired librarian, was the moderator. She banged a gavel and told Lucinda to lead off. As Snuffy had predicted, Lucinda clung to her lectern and read a prepared speech that outlined her platform of cuts.

"The money freed up could then be invested in more computers and courses in business, accounting, math, and science," she said. "Employers need young people with these skills. They do not need philosophers, poets, or oboe players. By making these changes we can lower taxes and maximize the financial return of the schools to the local economy."

Lucinda sat down to moderate applause. George abandoned his written speech and walked to the front of the stage.

"I'm not a philosopher, God knows. I'm not much of a poet, either, and I can't play the oboe, but I learned to appreciate poetry and literature and music in high school. That was fifty years ago, but I still remember how I felt when I discovered Wordsworth and Mark Twain and the *Jupiter* Symphony. Yes, students should be computer literate. But first, they should be literate in their native tongue, and in history and the arts.

"The trouble is," George continued, "whatever we teach is going to cost money. I'm not going to kid you—if the tax levy has to increase to keep our schools up to snuff, so be it. We owe it to the kids."

A shocked silence fell in the auditorium. The audience leaned forward and stared at George, sure that he had just committed political suicide before their eyes. Some smiled, some frowned. Betty Swain banged her gavel again. "How about some questions from the audience?" she said.

After a dozen predictable people had asked a dozen predictable questions, a tall man with a wrinkled neck and oversized, calloused hands stood up.

"My name is Nils Nilsson, and I farm up by Europe Lake," he said. "I have one question, and I would like both candidates to answer it in a minute or less. The question is, If you were on the school board, how would you measure success? You first, Lucinda."

"I would measure success by looking at the kids' paychecks after they graduate. The bigger the checks, the better their education has been."

"Well, I don't buy that at all," George responded. "First and foremost, kids have to be good citizens, which means they need to think for themselves, ask questions, and communicate. If they can do that, they've had a good education. They can learn a trade later."

"It sounds like George wants to create a lot of unemployed little liberals," Lucinda said. "Maybe he's a liberal himself. Maybe he'll spend us into the poorhouse like liberals usually do."

"You bet your bippy I'm a liberal, and proud of it." He turned toward the audience. "Who would you rather have on the school board—Bob Cratchit or Ebenezer Scrooge?" George asked.

"Sounds like socialism!" Lucinda hissed.

George raised his voice. "Socialism, my Aunt Fanny," he barked. "Lucinda, don't use big words you don't understand. You wouldn't know socialism if it bit you on the leg!"

"Gentlemen!" Betty Swain warned. "Or rather, gentleman and Lucinda. Let's be civil."

Helen raised her hand. "We're forgetting something," she said. "People aren't computers, and educating a child isn't like programming. No matter how much data you dump into it, a computer can't govern itself, or love poetry, or enjoy music, or tell right from wrong—only a human being can do that. An educated human being. Our parents weren't selfish—they paid their taxes and made sacrifices so we could go to good schools. Now it's time for us to make a few sacrifices for our kids."

Helen got more applause than George and Lucinda put together. Nils Nilsson stood up again.

"Who are you, lady?" he asked.

"My name is Helen O'Malley."

"Did you ever teach school?"

"Yes, I taught second grade for thirty-six years," replied Helen.

There was even more applause this time; members of the audience exchanged significant glances. Snuffy O'Toole was frowning; Tess Underwood was beaming. Betty Swain banged her gavel for the last time, and the debate was over. In the lobby, members of the high school orchestra handed out large four-color brochures with pictures of Helen and Russell on them, while a sophomore girl played Mozart on her oboe.

"Plan B?" George asked.

"Plan B," Helen replied. "Just to be on the safe side."

George got behind the wheel of Helen's old Buick and they headed for home. "Helen, you're the one with hidden depths. You were really eloquent."

"So were you, George. But somebody had to step in before you and Lucinda came to blows," Helen said. "She would have flattened you."

On election night, the Coot Lake neighbors gathered at Snuffy's to watch the returns. It was noisy and everyone was talking at once. At about ten o'clock, Snuffy handed George a cell phone. "A reporter wants to talk to you," he said. After a couple of minutes, George handed back the phone. There was an odd sort of smile on his face.

"Hey, Snuffy," he said, "switch the TV to channel five and get everybody to shut up, will ya?"

"Now here's an unusual story," the announcer said. "In the race for a seat on the Northern Door School Board, write-in candidate Helen O'Malley has defeated her husband, George O'Malley, by one vote, 257 to 256. Conservative candidate Lucinda Schmitz was a distant third with 117 votes. Moments ago, we contacted Mr. O'Malley by telephone, and he says he is retiring from politics and will not ask for a recount. Good thinking, George! And in other election news . . ."

At Snuffy's Tavern the following Tuesday night, the Bird and Booyah men were watching the Brewers while their wives watched reruns of *Dancing with Losers* at home.

"Whatever you do, George, don't show Helen how to record cable TV," said Bump. "I'm really getting to like Guinness."

Snuffy came over to their table and sat down. "Well, George, what's it like to have ED? Election dysfunction, I mean. Have you figured out why you lost?"

"Suppose you tell me," George said.

"All right—first off, Lucinda called you a liberal and you didn't deny it. The L-word is the kiss of death. That was strike one. Then you said you might have to raise taxes. Strike two. And finally, you lost your temper and yelled at Lucinda. Politicians today aren't supposed to have emotions or take issues to heart. So that was strike three and you were out. I'm surprised you got as many votes as you did."

George snorted. "Lucinda needed yelling at, and somebody had to do it. But I didn't lose, I won—big-time. Lucinda isn't on the school board, Helen is, and she's the one who has to go to all those meetings, not me. It worked out just like she and I planned it, with a little help from Tess."

Snuffy swallowed a mouthful of Guinness and coughed. "Do you mean to tell me that you planned that last-minute write-in business?"

"You bet. Some Door County voters are conservative, some are liberal, and some are in the middle—but they all understand the value of a dollar. They liked me well enough, but they liked Helen better. And when we offered them two roughly similar O'Malleys for the price of one, it was all over but the shouting."

Heine Lipschultz came in, weaving slightly, and sat at their table. "Whass up?" he asked.

"We were talking about the election," Bump said. "George was running for the school board, and Helen beat him by one vote."

"Hell, George, if I had known there was gonna be an election I woulda voted for you," Heine said.

"I'm glad you didn't," said George. "If Helen and I had tied, we'd have to start all over again. Life is too short for that.

"And God forbid, I might have won!"

The Last Summer

//

*G*eorge tied his rowboat to the dock and started up the path to the lodge, carrying a stringer of plump bluegills he had just caught in Coot Lake. It was early June, and the fish were starting to put on weight.

As he walked by Helen's old Buick station wagon, he heard a woman singing. He opened the driver's side door and turned the knob, but the radio was shut off.

"I guess it's Helen," he said. On the porch, he stopped to look and listen. Inside, in the light of the south windows, Helen was ironing and singing quietly to herself, while Russell slept at her feet.

"Well, she's in a good mood," George thought, and opened the screen door.

"Hey, kiddo, take a look," he said, holding up the stringer. "Nine of 'em, and they're all bigger than my hand. That's enough for supper."

"Great," said Helen. She beamed at George and shut off the iron. "But I've got some news that is better than bluegills. George, guess what! Josie and Bill called while you were out fishing, and we're going to be grandparents again, right around Thanksgiving! They didn't plan on it, but they're used to the idea now. And it's going to be a little girl."

"How do they know that?" George asked.

"Just take it on faith, George. They use a thing called ultrasound, and they can tell."

George took his bluegills into the kitchen, put them in the sink, and returned with two mugs of coffee. "Have they decided on a name?"

"Amy," Helen said. "Isn't that nice? It's got rhyme and rhythm—Amy O'Malley."

Helen chattered on about baby clothes and fixing up the nursery at Bill and Josie's house in Evanston. But George wasn't listening. He was looking out at the lake, sipping his coffee, and thinking about his ten-year-old grandson, Willie. He felt a pang of guilt.

"I haven't spent enough time with that boy," he thought, "and by Thanksgiving he'll have a little sister, and I'll have to divide my time between them. This will be our last summer together, just Willie and me."

After supper, they called Bill and Josie. When it was George's turn, he asked to talk to Willie.

"He isn't here, Dad," said Bill. "He's at a nature camp for a week."

"Nature camp? Why does he need a nature camp? He's got Door County!"

"Well, all his friends were going, and they teach the kids to swim and do crafts and things," Bill said. "Then after nature camp he's got a week of soccer camp, but he'll be able to come up there on the eighteenth."

"Fine," George said. "I'll bring him back around Labor Day."

When the phone call was over, George and Helen went out on the porch. George lit his pipe and looked at the western sky. But he wasn't able to enjoy the pipe or the sunset.

"Crafts!" he snorted. "The summer is galloping by and Willie is doing crafts, of all things. I went to a summer camp once where we did crafts. I made my dad a coin purse out of leather that was like cardboard, and it lasted about a week. Willie needs to learn practical things like fishing and bird watching and hitting curve balls.

"And ye Gods, a soccer camp?" George groaned. "Soccer is a game for scrawny little Europeans that kick each other in the shins and then roll around on the grass like they're at death's door. Bunch of play-actors. When a baseball player gets hit with a pitch, he just trots down to first like nothing happened. I'll bet those soccer players all throw like girls, and their brains are scrambled from bouncing the ball off their heads. They've got two perfectly good hands, so why don't they use 'em?"

"Well, soccer is what kids play these days," said Helen. "They learn teamwork, and it's aerobic."

"Phooey," George said. "Turning a double play is teamwork. Executing the run and hit is teamwork. And there's plenty of aerobics out in center field. Tomorrow, I'm going to go to Green Bay and buy Willie a good glove. I'll have two weeks to oil it and break it in."

"George, I know you want to teach Willie baseball and things," said Helen, "but when he gets here, don't overdo it, OK? Just let him unwind. Kids' lives are so organized—they go to school at the crack of dawn, and there are lessons for this and lessons for that. They hardly know how to play. Don't push."

As June slowly passed, George daydreamed happily about all the things he and Willie would do. But Helen was becoming concerned about Josie. They spoke on the phone almost every day.

"The doctor says there isn't anything really wrong," Helen said, "but she's sick every morning and just kind of tired out. She's thirty-five, it's been ten years since Willie was born, and she says she's lost the knack of being pregnant. She needs another woman to lean on, and now that her mother is gone and her women friends are all working, she's kind of alone."

George took charge. "Helen, when we go down to pick up Willie, you should stay there and help her. Willie and I can batch it up here, and that way Josie won't have to look after him."

"Could you do that, George? It would be a big help."

"No problem, and I'll have Willie all to myself for six weeks, maybe more. It works out all the way around."

That evening, when Helen was upstairs packing, George got a legal pad from a kitchen drawer, sat at the bar by the west windows, and started drawing up lists.

Things to Do
1. *Baseball*
2. *Fishing*

3. Sailing
4. Stone-skipping
5. Shooting BB gun and .22
6. Bird watching
7. Walks w/ Russell
8. Goofing off

Things to Buy
1. Baseballs
2. Bat
3. Rod and reel
4. BB gun
5. Binoculars
6 Bird book

Things to Eat and Drink
1. Milk
2. Eggs
3. Pancake mix
4. Maple syrup
5. Peanut butter
6. Chocolate ice cream
7. Watermelon
8. Wieners
9. Macaroni and cheese
10. Snickers

George reviewed his lists, looked at his reflection in the west windows, and smiled broadly at himself. His last summer with Willie was taking shape.

On the morning of the eighteenth of June, George paced up and down Bill and Josie's driveway, puffing impatiently on his pipe and waiting for his grandson. Helen came out of the house and stood next to him.

"Willie's bus should be here any minute, George. I can't wait to see him."

"Me neither," George said. "But listen, Helen, Willie and I will have to leave pretty quick if we're going to get back to Baileys Harbor at a reasonable hour. His stuff is all packed and loaded, so let's skip the tearful farewells, OK?"

"OK, Grandpa." She grinned at George and put her arm around his shoulders. "Before we got married, I guessed you would make a good grandfather, and I was right."

"Sizing me up even then, were you?"

"You don't know the half of it," Helen said.

Eventually they got going. Willie talked a blue streak while George drove, listened, and smiled. But by the time they got to the north side of Milwaukee, he was asleep.

"Poor kid is tuckered out," thought George. "They must have worked him pretty hard at those camps." Then, on an impulse, George took the Silver Spring exit and pulled into the parking lot of Kopp's Frozen Custard. Kopp's was one of his regular stops on the Evanston to Door County run.

Willie woke up when the car stopped moving. He yawned and stretched. "What's up, Grandpa?" he asked.

"Graduation day. From now on I'm going to call you Will. Willie is a little boy's name, and you aren't a little boy anymore. Do you think you could answer to Will?"

"All right, Grandpa—I will."

George laughed and punched Will gently in the shoulder. "Careful, kid," he said. "I still make the jokes around here. Let's go get you a graduation present."

Kopp's was busy, and George and Will had to wait in line. George ordered two chocolate malts, extra large and extra thick, and handed one to Will with a conspiratorial wink. "That is one of the little benefits of being on the loose with your grandfather."

"Jeez, Grandpa, Mom never lets me have stuff like this—she's worried that I'll get obese."

"Oh, let's risk it," said George. "You're so skinny I can practically see through you, and in any case you've got all summer to work it off."

"Yeah, I've got all summer, haven't I?"

Three hours later, George pulled off the highway and onto Coot Lake Road. He stopped at Bump and Emma's to pick up Russell, who greeted Will with ecstatic face licking and tail thrashing. Bump came out of the house and leaned in the window of the old Buick.

"Who's the handsome stranger?"

"His name used to be Willie, but now it's Will," George said. "Will O'Malley. How's that sound?"

"It's got a ring to it."

The next morning, George was up early. He put the coffee on, mixed up a bowl of pancake batter, and hollered up the stairs.

"Arise! Daylight in the swamp! The first pancake man will be ready in ten minutes!"

Nine minutes later, Will walked into the kitchen, his face still wet from a splash of water and a casual wipe with a washcloth. He looked at the pancake man on the griddle. "Hey, Grandpa, if I'm not a little boy, how come you're making me a pancake man?"

"You never outgrow your need for pancake men," replied George. "The next one is mine."

After Will's third pancake man had been washed down by a dollar's worth of maple syrup, George poured himself another cup of coffee. "Will, go into the living room and fetch what you will find on the mantel over the fireplace."

Will was back in a minute with a Wilson A2000 glove smelling of neat's-foot oil, and a bag of baseballs. "Those are yours, Will. Would you like to play catch?"

Out in the yard, George studied the mechanics of Will's throwing motion. Then he held Will's arm and moved it through a proper baseball throw. "Drop your arm behind you, then rotate it. Stride forward with your left foot, come right over the top, and flip the ball off your fingers with a snap of the wrist. Keep that up and you'll have a major league arm, like me."

They tossed the ball back and forth for a half hour. But George remembered Helen's warning: "Let him unwind. Don't push."

"That's enough, Will," he said. "Your old grandpa's major league arm is getting tired."

After lunch, Will looked around the lodge for something to do. "We don't have any video games," George said, "but there's a nice breeze and Bump has a little sailboat we can borrow—he keeps it at his father's cottage on Clark Lake. Hop in the truck and we'll give it a try."

At the lake, they put on life jackets, raised the jib and mainsail, and lowered the centerboard. George paddled the boat out far enough to catch the breeze, and within a minute they were bounding along downwind. As they approached the far side of the lake, George jibed and began to tack upwind. With the breeze blowing across their faces, the boat seemed to be going even faster, and occasional gusts leaned it over.

"Sit on the windward gunwale when she heels like that. Otherwise we could capsize."

"Grandpa, I don't know what you're talking about," said Will, speaking loudly to be heard over the crackling of the sail, the hiss of the wake alongside, and the pattering of the bow as it cut through the waves.

When they returned to their starting point, George came about and made room for Will on the stern seat.

"OK, you take her downwind for a while. Hold the tiller in your left hand and the mainsheet in your right, like this, steer for that brown boathouse over there, and haul in on the sheet to harden up the sail if it flaps."

Will laughed in sheer delight at the little boat's speed. "I still don't know what you're talking about, Grandpa, but this is great."

On their third downwind run, George slacked the main boom all the way to starboard and rigged the jib to port. "You call this sailing at a broad reach, wing on wing," he said. "Isn't it pretty?"

The breeze held all afternoon, and they sailed for five hours nonstop. By late afternoon Will knew loo'ard from windward, port from starboard, the difference between coming about and jibing, and how to handle the tiller and mainsheet.

He also learned the hard way that heeling meant tipping over, and that if a boat heeled too far, it would capsize. But it was only a minor capsize in four feet of water, the sort of thing that could happen to anybody, and they were already wet through from the spray. They righted the boat, climbed back aboard, bailed her out, and kept on sailing. "Now you know why I locked my wallet in the truck," George said.

As the setting sun dipped into the treetops, George reached the end of their last downwind run, rounded her up, and headed the boat into the failing breeze.

"Tack her back to the dock, O Admiral of the Ocean Sea," he said. "If the wind drops much more we'll be becalmed."

"Aye-aye," said Will O'Malley.

After they had tied up the little boat, they furled her sail and stood looking at the expanse of Clark Lake as its light-green water turned purple in the twilight.

"'There is nothing—absolutely nothing—half so much worth doing as simply messing about in boats,'" George said. "That's from a book called *The Wind in the Willows*. Remind me to buy you a copy."

And so the summer went on. There was more sailing, and games of catch every day, and once or twice a week something new would appear on the mantel—a bat, a fishing rod, a BB gun, books, and binoculars—and there would be new things to do and learn.

But sometimes they just goofed off. One day they drove up to Northport to watch the Washington Island ferry come and go, and to hunt for flat stones on the beach. They threw the stones sidearm to see how many times they could make them skip. Will threw a couple that skipped five times, but George was the champion with a magnificent eleven.

One morning in mid-July they had glazed doughnuts for breakfast. Will dunked one of his doughnuts in a cup of milky coffee George had poured for him, and bit off a piece.

"What are we going to do today, Grandpa?" Will asked.

"Why don't we take the johnboat and stick our nose up the Mink River? It's a pretty place, and there used to be big pike and smallmouth in there when I was your age. Make us some lunch while I hitch the trailer to the truck."

The johnboat was in the water within an hour, and George's old ten-horse Elgin started on the first pull. They were motoring slowly across Rowleys Bay toward the mouth of the river when the Elgin began to miss and sputter. Then it quit running altogether.

George lifted the gas tank. "Plenty of gas," he said. "Whatever is wrong, I'd better fix it quick—that northwest wind will blow us out into Lake Michigan, and it's choppy out there. It will be a long, wet row back to the landing if I can't get this thing to run."

He disconnected the hose between the gas tank and the motor. "Sometimes these fittings and O-rings get dirty, and the motor winds up sucking more air than gas." He wiped off both ends of the hose with his handkerchief, but the motor still wouldn't start.

"I suppose it could be the plugs," said George. He tipped up the motor, removed the cowling, unscrewed both spark plugs, and looked them over. "They aren't fouled, and I'm running out of things to fix. If it's the coil or the points or the condenser, we're in real trouble. So I'm going to assume the carburetor jets are dirty. Will, hand me the toolbox from the rod locker."

George partially disassembled the carburetor. Then he took a pipe cleaner from his tobacco pouch and stripped off its fuzz with his pocketknife. They were drifting into rougher water, the boat was bouncing around, and it was getting difficult to work while bent over the transom.

"Say a little prayer, Will," he said, and began poking the pipe cleaner wire into the jets. "This will either kill it or cure it."

After a minute of poking he reassembled the carburetor and tipped the motor back down. He squeezed the bulb to pump in some fresh gas and pulled the starter rope. The motor started and idled down to a confident purr. "Thank God," George sighed. "Let's get out of this wind and go fishing."

The Mink River was still beautiful, but the fishing was slow. At noon, George nosed the johnboat into some reeds along the shore and opened the lunch Will had packed for him: a peanut butter sandwich, a Snickers bar, and a Coke. He had finished the sandwich and was sleepily gnawing at the Snickers when he heard a voice behind him, so close that it made his hair stand on end.

"Say, you fellows, could you give us a tow? Both of my batteries are dead and the motor won't start."

George turned and saw a man about his own age and a boy about Will's age, standing in a twenty-foot bass boat with Illinois numbers. It was drifting slowly down the river. The man had a thick head of silver hair and a deep golfer's tan, and wore a white cashmere sweater with a little alligator sewn on it.

"No trouble at all," said George. He pushed the johnboat out of the reeds with an oar and tossed the man a length of rope. "It'll take a while, but we'll get you back."

At the landing, George backed his trailer down the ramp and quickly loaded his boat, so that the alligator man would have room to load his. George bent down and whispered to Will. "I've got to piss like a racehorse. Keep an eye on the truck and the boat. I'll be back in a minute."

When George came out of the men's room, he could see that the alligator man was having trouble backing his boat trailer down the ramp. He jackknifed it to the right, then to the left, and to the right again, growing angrier at each attempt. George walked over to the alligator man's giant SUV and tapped on the window.

"Why don't you let me have a go at it? You're going to damage your trailer." George climbed behind the wheel and backed the big trailer down the ramp, dead center on the first try. He turned on the electric winch, hooked the cable to the boat, and pulled it on the trailer.

The alligator man shook George's hand. Then he reached for his wallet. "Let me pay you something for your trouble."

"No, it was no trouble at all. You would do the same for me."

The alligator man looked surprised. "Well—thank you."

"You're welcome."

George leaned against the gunwale of his boat and scowled. He was angry with himself.

"That guy offered me money because I look like I'm broke," he thought. "I spent thirty years working for peanuts, and now I'm paying the price. Hell, if I had any gumption I could have earned some real money at an ad agency. Then it would be me with the bass boat, and me with the big car and the cashmere sweater—not that I would wear the wussy-looking thing.

"But instead, the best I can do is a ten-year-old truck and a twenty-year-old boat and a thirty-year-old outboard that I have to fix every other time I use it. I'm an embarrassment to myself. What do people think of me? Most important, what does Will think of me?"

George popped the top of the warm can of Coke from his lunch bag and drank a couple of swallows. Then he heard the high-pitched voice of the boy from the bass boat. He was talking to Will.

"That's a neat boat you got. If you and your Grandpa hadn't been there, we'd be halfway to Michigan by now. And your Grandpa sure can back up a trailer."

"And," Will said, "my grandpa can fix an outboard motor with a pipe cleaner and sail a sailboat and shift gears and tie flies . . . and . . ."

"And what?"

"And he can make a stone skip eleven times!"

"Eleven times? Really?"

"Really. He did it just the other day."

"Wow! That's something!" the boy said. "My grandpa can only get three skips. Well, see ya around."

"Yeah, see ya."

George felt a lot better. "Out of the mouths of babes and sucklings," he thought.

He tightened the tie-down strap on the johnboat, got behind the wheel of his truck, and started the engine. "Come on, Will, let's hit the road," he said.

"Where are we going, Grandpa?"

"Oh, I don't know. What do you say we go up to Northport and skip stones?"

When George and Will got back to the lodge in the late afternoon, the phone was ringing. George ran into the kitchen and hit the speaker button. Bill, Josie, and Helen started singing.

> Happy birthday to you,
> Happy birthday to you.
> Happy birthday, dear Geo-orge,
> Happy birthday to you!

"Good grief, it's my birthday," replied George. "I completely forgot about it. Old-timers' disease has claimed another victim. How are things down there?"

"Josie is doing fine," Helen said. "But we still have plenty to do—we haven't even started painting the nursery, so I'll have to stay for a couple of weeks yet. How are you and Willie getting along?"

"You mean Will," George said. "His name is Will now. We're doing fine too, and he is straightening me out on a number of things."

George made wieners and macaroni for supper. When they were finished eating, Will brought in a brown paper lunch bag. "Happy birthday, Grandpa," he said.

George reached into the bag and pulled out a hand-tooled tobacco pouch, a small, flat one to hold his flake tobacco.

"I made it at camp, Grandpa," Will said. "It's genuine leather and I stamped your initials on it. It's got rubber inside and a pocket for pipe cleaners."

"Oh, yes, you always need pipe cleaners," said George. "Especially when you have an old Elgin." He hugged Will and found it difficult to swallow. "Thanks," he said.

"No trouble at all," Will replied.

"Now, where have I heard that before?" George thought.

A few days later, George and Will returned from an afternoon of sailing and were surprised to find that the lodge was almost hidden behind a wall of parked cars. When they ventured inside they heard a clatter of pans and occasional profanity from the kitchen. The Baileys Harbor Bird and Booyah Club was catering their supper. "I hope you two are hungry," said Bump. "Emma made a three-story chocolate cake, Jack brought about a cubic foot of Rosa's lasagna, Lloyd is thawing out a gallon of the booyah we made in May, and Leroy is broiling venison burgers."

"And you don't have to worry about this venison," Leroy said. "It's bran' fresh. I hit it myself Tuesday night on Plum Bottom Road."

"Wonderful," said George, "but what's the occasion?"

"Tonight we initiate the first junior member of the Bird and Booyah Club," Hans explained. "Somebody named Will."

When supper was over and the lasagna had been reduced to a shadow of its former self, Lloyd placed a chair in front of the fireplace. "Sit down, Will, and the rest of you, sit on the couches and witness the initiation."

"I will ask you four questions," Lloyd said. "And you must answer each of them truthfully. Question number one—who is the best fisherman you know?"

"Grandpa."

"And the best sailor?"

"Grandpa."

"And the best birdwatcher?"

"Grandpa."

"And who do you know that never tells a lie?"

"Grandpa," Will replied, without a second of hesitation.

There was a moment of silence.

"Well, three out of four ain't bad," said Deputy Doug. "He lied like a trouper on that last one, but what matters is loyalty, and he's got that in spades. I move that we accept Will O'Malley as a junior member."

"Second!" they all said.

"All those in favor signify in the usual manner—"

"AYE!"

"Opposed? Sensing none, the motion is carried. Welcome aboard."

Everyone but George applauded. He blew his nose noisily and dabbed at the corners of his eyes with his handkerchief.

Hans slapped George on the back. "Let's eat the cake and ice cream before George Washington here gets all misty. George, do you want to cut the cake?"

"I'll do it with my little hatchet," replied George.

Later that evening, George and Will watched a movie on television. George filled his new tobacco pouch with Irish Flake. When the movie was over, he stood up and yawned.

"I don't know about you, but I'm going to hit the sack," he said. "Let's go fishing in the morning."

George slept a little late, and it was about seven thirty when Will hollered up the stairs.

"Arise! Daylight in the swamp! The bluegills are biting, and I've got three already!"

"Last summer, hell," George thought. "With any luck, this is just the beginning."

The Return of Tuddy

///

It was the Saturday after Thanksgiving, and Chicago was living up to its reputation. A thin mixture of rain and snow pattered on the windows of the maternity ward waiting room, and a twenty-mile-an-hour wind rattled the sash.

George and Helen held hands and watched their son, Bill, pace up and down. Somewhere down the hall, Josie was in labor.

"I don't know what to think," Bill said. "She was having a rough time and then they shooed me out of the room. Something must be wrong."

Helen walked to the door. "I'll go and ask the nurse."

"For God's sake, Bill, sit down and take a load off," George suggested, after Helen had left. "They always have a rough time, but things usually work out."

"Yeah, usually, but not always. I'm scared, Dad."

"Bill, do you realize that you were born in this same hospital, and that I paced up and down in this same waiting room?" George said. "In those days, there were ashtrays overflowing with cigarette butts in here, and smoke as thick as fog in February. There was another guy waiting and chain-smoking Chesterfields. When he ran out he smoked all the butts that were long enough to light, and when those were gone, he asked me if he could borrow my pipe."

Bill smiled and sat down next to George. "You never told me that one, Dad. What happened?"

"Well, I filled it for him, and he finally got it lit—but then he inhaled and got sick."

"That's what happened when I tried to smoke your pipe when I was about sixteen," Bill said. He stood up and started pacing again.

George looked at his watch. "Excuse me for a minute, I've got to make a call." He stepped out into the hall and dialed a number on his cell phone.

"Could I speak to the doctor, please?" he said. "Hello, Doc. You'd better give me the bad news first. How serious is it?"

Someone spoke on the other end of the line.

"Well, that's pretty much what I expected. Thanks. I'm tied up now, but I'll get there as soon as I can—maybe later this afternoon."

Helen returned from down the hall. "Josie will be going into the delivery room any minute," she said to Bill. "If you want to see her first you should do it now."

"Come with me, Mom," Bill said. "They told me I could go into the delivery room with her, but I've got to scrub up and put on a gown, and I'll need you to tie it in back."

They started down the hallway together, but Bill stopped and gripped Helen's hand. "I don't need you to tie my gown. Mom, is Dad OK?"

"As far as I know," said Helen. "What's the trouble?"

"He doesn't know it, but I just overheard him on the phone. He was talking to a doctor, and it didn't sound good. And you remember, yesterday afternoon he took off in the car and wouldn't say where he was going. As if we haven't got enough on our plates already!"

"Oh," Helen said, and frowned. "Well, you worry about Josie and I'll worry about your father."

Back in the waiting room, George dialed the same number again.

"Doc? George O'Malley. On second thought, I'm not going to be able to get down there today. Would you mind billing me? My address is on the card I left. And would you put it in a cab? Evanston Memorial, care of George O'Malley. Not Bill or Helen—George. Thanks."

George stationed himself by the waiting room window. In about a half hour, a cab pulled up in front of the hospital, and the driver got out, carrying a paper bag. George walked to the bank of elevators. In a few minutes, he returned with the bag, just as an obstetrics nurse bustled by.

"You're a grandfather," she said. "Ten fingers, ten toes, everybody's OK. You'll be able to see Mom and the baby in a little while."

When George and Helen were finally ushered into Josie's room, young Amy was sound asleep, red faced and puffy eyed and beautiful. "Do you want to hold her for a while, Helen?" Josie said.

"I thought you'd never ask. And now, George, will you please tell us what's wrong? We know you were talking to a doctor. We're going to find out sooner or later, and we can't enjoy the baby for worrying about you."

"Oh, for cripes sake," George said. "I should have known it's impossible to keep a secret in this family. I'm not the patient, Tuddy is." He reached into the paper bag and pulled out a worn but serviceable brown teddy bear about a foot long.

"This is Tuddy. That's what I named him when I was two. I found him in the attic a couple of weeks ago and thought I would give him to Amy, but he was pretty dirty, and his stuffing was coming out, and worst of all, he had lost an eye. I figured a one-eyed teddy bear would give the baby nightmares.

"Then I remembered a little shop in the Loop—Doctor John's Doll Clinic, it's called. So I dropped Tuddy off yesterday for emergency treatment. They cleaned him up and replaced his innards and found an eye just like the one he had lost.

"I called the clinic this afternoon to find out if he was done and how much it would cost. He doesn't have Medicare, so it was plenty, and that was the bad news. I had them deliver him in a cab. He's still a little shabby, but after all, he's sixty-nine. Have you got your camera, Bill? Take a picture of Amy and Tuddy."

That evening, George was sitting at Bill and Josie's kitchen table, criticizing the front page layout of the *Chicago Tribune* while Helen took sheets of sticky buns out of the oven. Will was sitting at the opposite side of the table, drinking a glass of milk and reading *The Wind in the Willows*.

"What do you think of your little sister, Will?" George asked.

"She's pretty and she has blue eyes and a nice smile," Will said. "Just like Grandma."

George laughed. "There speaks a true O'Malley. He's kissed the blarney stone, that one!"

"What's it like to be a grandpa again, George?" Helen asked.

"To tell you the truth, it makes me feel kind of old. Happy, but old."

"Don't get old before I do, George," said Helen, and gave him a kiss. "You're still my sweetheart, and you're still the best-looking Irishman in Door County. And don't you forget it."

Will looked up from his book and snickered. "You guys are funny."

"You bet," George said.

"Lucky, too."

AUTHOR'S NOTE

Like Guy Noir, Garrison Keillor's private eye, I'm still searching for the answers to life's persistent questions—such as, what happened to the apostrophe in Baileys Harbor?

"Baileys" is a possessive and there ought to be an apostrophe, but there isn't. What happened to it? It's a mystery. All we can say is that Baileys Harbor has been spelled that way for more than 160 years and isn't likely to change.

We do know that there was a Captain Justice Bailey, and that in 1848 he hove to in a storm on Lake Michigan and took shelter in an uncharted bay, saving a schooner-load of immigrants from discomfort and possible drowning. The next morning he went ashore, discovered vast stands of timber and deposits of limestone, and named the bay after himself.

I suspect we'll never find out where the apostrophe went, or if there ever was one. In the grand scheme of things, it doesn't matter much. But there is a certain satisfaction in knowing that "Baileys" is correct, and "Bailey's" is not.

Blessed are we whose pleasures are simple, right?